3 1526 05321134 5

W9-BLU-402

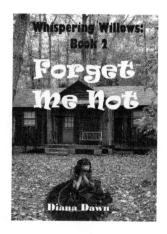

Your FREE book is waiting!

"Forget Me Not"...After falling into a magical world called the Whispering Willows, Snow has found new friends and her "Prince Charming". But her wicked stepmother is still after her. If she is to find any peace in her new life, she must find a way to destroy the evil witch...a way that will not endanger her new friends or herself in the process. "Forget Me Not" is the second book in the Whispering Willows series.

Get a FREE copy of the next book in the exciting Whispering Willows series and see what happens next!

Just visit: www.DianaDawnBooks.com/free

Whispering Willows Book 1: "Fallen Snow"

by Diana Dawn

Chapter 1
"Fallen Snow"

"Run! Hide in the woods! Never come back, or she'll kill you!"

These words kept booming in her head like a crash of thunder. Never had she run so fast. It was pure adrenaline that kept Snow's tiny feet running as fast as they could away from the huntsman. It was only his sincere devotion to the little princess that kept him from killing her at the evil queen's demand. "Why?" Snow thought. What had she done? She was faithful to her many chores and polite to her stepmother. And to never return? Where would she go? She had never ventured very far from her own castle home. And she was surely approaching the enchanted forest, a place she had been warned against time and again ... a place of mystery and doom, she had been told. Yet, she had to keep running ... to where, she did not know. The fear in her eyes turned to grief and as the tears streamed down her face, she wished her father were still alive to comfort her, to hold her.

"Daddy!" She yelled as she kept running ... but to no avail. There was nothing around her, but the trees and the vines that now began to appear menacing and started to grab at her ankles and tear at her dress. The fact that her favorite dress was being tattered did not even cross her mind. She had no family, no friends even, except the servants with whom she shared chores with. For so long, she had dreamt of her handsome prince, that he would come and carry her off to his castle to live happily ever after. This dream seemed so far away now, as she grew weary from running but did not dare stop. The shadows growing darker, now seemed to reach out to grab her. At times, they made her jump aside, sometimes tripping over branches and brush. So scared now, Snow leapt from one of the menacing shadows falling into a brush. Instead of a grounding, she found herself sliding through a deep chasm below the brush's disguise. She screamed, frantically grabbing at anything and everything her fingers could find. But the moss and dirt delivered no rescue from what seemed like an eternal fall. She saw what she thought was light growing closer, rushing towards her feet. At that moment, her feet broke through a wall of branches and into a padded pile of what felt like leaves, and her fall had come to a stop.

Thank God, she thought. At that second, a rain of the branches she had just broken through began to fall all around her, and after a painful thump on her head, Snow's world went black.

When she slowly opened her eyes, Snow found herself still surrounded with the leaves she had fallen into. She moved her hands, but there was something different, here. She looked down ... a blanket! She was covered with a blanket. What was this? Where did it come from? It wasn't one from her own castle homestead. Quickly she sat up, her head now throbbing with pain from where the branch crashed down on her.

She grabbed her head, "Ouch. Hello?" She called to anyone. "Is anyone there? Hello!"

"Hello", a male voice said back to her. Coming out from his hiding place in the bushes was a tall gentleman who wore a black shiny coat and a look of genuine concern. "There now, you 'ave a nasty bump. That's why your 'ead 'urts." This man talked rather strangely. It took Snow an extra second to decipher all of what he said. "Took a bad fall ya did. Did ya fall off'n yer horse?"

From the words "fall" and "horse", Snow gathered that the young man had asked her if she had 'fallen off of her horse'. "No", she replied back, never removing her hand from the throbbing spot on her head.

He could see fear in her eyes, but not fear of him. He saw a fear that she possessed as soon as she awoke to recall where she was and how she got there. "M' name's Stevie" as he helped her to her feet.

"Good day, Stevie. My name is Snow", she said in the polite way in which she was instructed at the palace.

Stevie recognized the style and accent in her voice to match closely that of Ivan and was slightly relieved. She seemed very young to him, possessing an innocence that attracted him to her all the more. He felt a desperate desire to protect this lovely young girl from whatever brought her here. "Well, Snow. We should get ya back to the village an' get some ice fer yer 'ead there. Don't want it to swell up any worse now. 'Ow did ya fall and 'urt yer 'ead?"

Snow handed him the blanket, "Well, it's a rather long story."

Stevie smiled excitedly, "At's alright. We have a way's to go back to the Willows."

"What's the Willows?" Snow asked with some concern in her voice.

"At's where we live. Me and my friends. Don't worry, they are very nice, most of 'em. You shouldn't 'ave any problems. 'Ow did you get 'ere, Snow? We don't get many visitors, and the ones we get usually can't remember 'ow they got 'ere any'ow."

"Well, " Snow began slowly, as if trying to remember clearly, "I was running from the huntsman who had orders from my stepmother to have me killed. As I was running through the forest, I fell into some kind of deep hole, or something, and ended up here."

Stevie had stopped and turned to her, "Wait a minute, you're teasing wit' me aren't you? Name's Snow, runnin' from a huntsman, stepmother trying to kill ya? C'mon. What really happened to ya?"

Snow backed away from him. "I am telling you what happened. Are you calling me a liar?"

Stevie's smile disappeared. He didn't mean to upset this girl, but he really thought she was putting him on. "Sorry, ya mean 't's what really 'appened?"

Snow nodded.

"Wow! I can't believe this, it's a like a reg'lar like fairy tale this is! So that must mean you're a princess, right?"

Snow's doe-eyed expression became even wider. "Yes, but how did you know that?"

He grabbed her hand, "C'mon, I can't wait to tell the others!" He quickened their pace.

Puzzled, Snow offered, "Tell the others about what?"

But Stevie was already lost in his own excitement in bringing Snow to Whispering Willows. It was like he was bringing his own personal fairy tale to their world, something he thought the village needed. In turn, Snow was intrigued by this stranger pulling her through the woods. He possessed an excitement about life that she thought was a rare sight to behold. She pondered back to her dreams of her handsome prince, and realized what a strange resemblance this young man had to the prince in her dreams ... she just noticed that! Although, his nature reminded her more of her favorite servant playmate since childhood, in any case, she thought to herself that this man could be the makings of a very good friend.

"OK, so how much more do we have to cut?" Murray inquired to Roger as he looked down at the lumber they had been cutting for the new rabbit pen they were planning to build.

"Probably about twice that amount", Roger replied back as he eyed the stack of wood.

"Well for Pete's sake, Roger, how many rabbits are we planning to have?"

"Murray, have you ever seen a litter of rabbits? Believe me, you've never seen so many babies come out of one creature. Besides, it seems like lately we have been adding a new mouth to feed around here every day. We will need as much meat as we can get."

As Murray was about to leave for more wood, he caught a glimpse of Stevie heading their direction. "Oh good God!" Murray exclaimed as he realized Stevie was not approaching with a familiar face.

Roger rolled his eyes at this friend's reluctance, "Murray,

quit your belly-aching and let's just go get some more wood."

Murray motioned to Stevie "No, not that, THAT!!"

Roger dropped the piece of lumber he had been inspecting. "Well, what do you know about that, another mouth to feed. Next time I'll be sure and keep my mouth shut!"

"Hey, guys!" Stevie cried, "look wha' I found in the woods. Those are some woods, aren't they? This is Snow. Snow, this is Murray and Roger."

Snow found herself face to face with two other men that looked practically identical to her guide, had it not been for the differences in clothing and hair. And once again, each man looked like the prince in her dreams, her prince. But how could this be possible? Besides, she only needed one, not three!

Getting a second look at the lovely young stranger, the two men were not as disheartened as before. "Hello miss," said Murray with a nod of his head.

"A pleasure," stated Roger as he took Snow's hand and kissed it.

She smiled. As the two gentlemen kept their glance on her for what seemed to be an unusually long time, Snow became somewhat nervous.

"What's this, or shall I say WHO is this?" came the booming voice of Ivan. His tone hinted on the 'flirtatious' as he approached the rest of the group.

Eghad, thought Snow, now there are four!

"Ivan, this is Snow. She's a new friend, so we need to treat her right, ya know. I found 'er knocked out cold in the woods. She took a nasty fall, she did."

"Well, Stevie, it appears you have found an enchanting friend, indeed." And then with a bow, "Wilfred of Ivanhoe at your service."

Ivanhoe had, just like the others, stumbled into the Willows magically. But he was from a different point in history. He was from the twelfth century, a time of chivalry along with betrayal.

"But you can call him Ivan ... the girls call him both, depending on their mood." chuckled Stevie.

"Girls?" Snow inquired eager to find companionship, even safety, amongst a female group.

Stevie's eyes lit up "Oh yes! You have to come and meet the girls, I know they'll love you!"

At which point Murray leaned in to Roger, "Let's HOPE they do, that is."

Roger offered back, "Nah, it doesn't matter as long as we do, eh?" Both laughed as Stevie led, or truth be said, pulled the clueless girl toward the huts.

"This material is just too ... what's the word here? Frilly! That's it, it's too frilly", complained Jill as she inspected the bag of material Kate had brought into the cabin.

"Well, I thought it was rather pretty" offered Kate as she spread her hand across a pink silken remnant.

"Me too", offered Kristen.

"Yeah, it's pretty but ... I'm sorry, Kate. I didn't mean to complain. I'm sure it will be good for something." Jill sighed.

Kristen offered, "It's just not something you go ridin' in or anything like that, that's all."

Kate put the material back in the bag. "Well, I'll agree with you there. I suppose it would make some nice curtains, though. I still get self-conscious at night wondering who may be walking by and looking in the windows."

Jill laughed, "Amen to that!"

As the women heard a rap at the window, they looked over to see Stevie peering in at them smiling and waving. All three of them laughed.

"Case in point!" managed Kristen as she went to the door.

Without even a knock or a hello, Stevie burst through the door just as Kristen reached for the handle. "Hey, I got someone for ya t' meet."

To all of their shock, Stevie pulled in a woman. She was quite young-looking with very light skin, almost pale, but a soft look. She had large blue eyes and dark brown hair, which had soft curls and just slightly brushed across her shoulders. She wore a medieval style outfit ... a burgundy blouse with puffy sleeves, royal blue lace-up top, and a yellow tattered skirt bottom. She looked like she just stepped out of a fairy tale costume contest, frankly, thought Jill. Adding to her youthful look was the ribbon in her hair and her 'doe-eyed' facial expression.

"Well glory be ... another woman! Thank heaven!", Kate praised.

Jill eyed her curiously, "Where in the world did ya come from, child? You look like you just fell outta Disneyland or something."

Snow look puzzled, "Fell from where?"

Stevie offered his own, "Oh no, Jill! She did fall, but she fell down this deep 'ole, wasn't it Snow? Then she go' knocked out cold down th' woods. I found her. She was runnin' fer her life, she was."

"Running for her life?" repeated Kate with much concern.

"Well", began Snow but was innocently interrupted by the rest of Stevie's version.

"Yeah, ya see, Snow's stepmother got this huntsman fellow to try an' kill her, see. But he let her go, probably 'coz she's so beautiful," with a glance at Snow, she blushed. "Then he told her to run into th' woods an' never return. She can't even go back 'ome, see?"

Kristen was taking in the conversation as if she had a notepad in her hand ... in fact, she wished she had, avid writer that she was.

Jill giggled, "Oh Stevie, she's puttin' one over on ya, boy. You're a sweetheart, but ya believe everything ya hear."

Snow frowned, and with a pout in her lips the disappointment in her voice was obvious, "Why is it that no one in this village seems to believe me? I was not brought up to tell lies!" With tears in her eyes, she brushed passed the group and went out the door. She stopped on the steps, as she wiped her tears and tried not to cry. Where was this place? She just wanted to go home, but she couldn't. She wanted her father back, but she couldn't have that either.

Stevie looked at Jill, "Oh, now look, you've gone and made 'er cry, Jill. Why'd ya do that?"

Jill's smile left her face, "I'm sorry Stevie, I didn't realize. Does she actually believe those things?"

Stevie nodded, "Yes, because they're true."

Before Jill could reply, Kate offered, "Jill, you know anything can happen here. Remember where we are, what we've seen? Nothing surprises me anymore."

Jill nodded, "Yes, that's true. Sorry, Stevie. Let's go talk to her."

The four of them headed outside and Kristen quickly glanced around the room as a last ditch effort to find a pen and paper.

"Rein, you're going to eat all of them. There won't be enough for the pies!" Mitch and Rein came into view of the cottages with Mitch carrying a large basket of berries and Rein tossing one after another into the air and catching them in his mouth.

"Well, there were plenty more back there. You could always go pick more later if need be."

He smiled mischievously as Mitch rolled his eyes. "Thanks a lot."

Rein stopped as they came in view of Jill's porch, "Whoa, what do we have here? I can't believe it. It looks like another lovely guest to the Willows."

Mitch looked in the same direction as Rein and almost dropped his basket as he set it down. The two of them approached the gang on the porch.

Stevie spotted them and smiled with delight. "Aye! Mitch and Rein, this is Snow."

Mitch was about to take her hand when Rein beat him to the punch. He took her hand and kissed it, "A pleasure."

In seeing the two men, Snow had to blink her eyes a few times. Here again were more of these 'look-alike' gentlemen. The one called 'Mitch' was just a little chubbier than the one called 'Rein', and they all had different hairstyles and clothing styles. But still, they all looked alike. What kind of village was this? It was like there were all of these 'twins'. Snow had only seen one set of twins in her life. The two sons of Lord Chamberlain were twins, and she found the concept fascinating. But it was nearly impossible to tell those two boys apart. So this predicament she found herself in today was quite peculiar. What was even more curious is that each and every one of these gentlemen looked just like the prince, the one she keeps dreaming about. Oh, of course ... that was it! That MUST be it! This was all a dream! She was going to wake up any minute in her own bed in her own castle and all of this will have been a dream. A thought which now seemed to almost sadden her, as she thought this village filled with would-be 'prince look-alikes' was something she found most interesting. But alas, she also found comfort in thinking that at any given moment she would awaken in her own bed.

Stevie continued, "I found her in the woods. She 'ad a nasty fall. She was runnin' from..."

Kate interrupted him "It's a long story. Why don't we get everybody together for dinner and we can all hear the story then, mmm? Sound good? Mitch, can you make one of your most famous dishes? Us girls will get Snow cleaned up for dinner."

Stevie offered quickly, "We need t' get some ice for her 'ead, 'ere." He pointed to where the lump on her head was without touching it.

"All right, what's this? We 'ave another female in our midst, do we?"

Stevie's face lit up as Donnie walked up to the group. While his tone gave off an approval to having another female in the village, his look was that of skepticism.

Kristen frowned. She didn't think Donnie would accept her story very graciously and feared for Snow regarding the consequences. "Donnie, this is Snow."

Donnie eyed her up and down, "Why, she's just a kid."

Snow protested, "I turned nineteen years the last moon."

Donnie never took his gaze off her as if he were interrogating her with his eyes. "What's her story?"

Stevie began his excited tone once again, "She took a bad fall in th' woods and I had to nurse her back. She was knocked out cold." Before anyone could stop him, Stevie proceeded to tell Donnie Snow's whole story. Why not? Donnie was his good friend. Why shouldn't he believe Stevie?

Donnie's face wore a combination of disbelief and laughter. "You've got to be kidding me? You don't actually believe this, do ya?"

Upon hearing another doubter to her story, Snow dropped her eyes and again the pout returned to her lips. Rein and Mitch both found this innocent look to be most appealing. Rein was especially aware of the red full lips that formed that innocent pout.

Stevie approached him, "Donnie, it's true."

"Yeah, and I'm the king of England!"

Snow looked up upon hearing this and her eyes it up again, "Really, my father was the King of the House of White!"

Stevie was enlightened with a revelation, "Aye! See, she is Snow White!"

Donnie rolled his eyes. Snow's face was one of relief in hearing someone finally believed her. She smiled at Stevie. Why were the others having such a hard time? Perhaps they were used to lying gypsies coming through their village. She hoped she never ran into any of them. Just then she felt someone grab her arm.

Donnie was pulling her down the porch steps. "All right then, Snow White. Maybe you'll tell us where you REALLY came from with a little interrogation. Perhaps with a little trip to the jail, maybe?" As he pulled her down the last step, Snow lost her footing and fell to the ground, with Donnie's hand still firmly and painfully grasping her arm.

"Donnie, stop please! You're hurting her! She's my friend, Donnie!" Stevie pleaded as he saw the painful look in her eyes.

"We need to find out more about her, Stevie. We can't just take her word at face value, ya know."

Kate stepped down to Donnie, "Let her go, Donnie." She was stern, even though Donnie was her lover, "She's just a child, you said so yourself!"

"Yeah, well kids can be strong. Let's find out how strong this kid really is!" He reached down with his other hand and squeezed her face, causing her lips to protrude in an involuntary pout.

Snow was terrified. She didn't know what to think of this 'barbarian', who again, possessed the look of the other men. But this one was rough and had cold eyes that pierced right through her soul, sending a shiver down her spine. Why was he so vicious? What had she done? Trying to think of anything to get away from this barbarian who threatened to take her away to wherever, she grabbed a handful of dirt with her free arm and flung it into her captor's face.

Letting go of the girl he violently rubbed his eyes, "Sod it!", he yelled!

Snow had scampered to her feet, pushed through Mitch and Rein and made a beeline for the woods.

"Snow!" Stevie cried, "Wait!" He went after her, as did the girls.

"Why didn't you two grab her?" Donnie shouted at Mitch and Rein as they stood there, speechless.

As Donnie ran after the others, Rein offered "Man, let her go! She's an innocent child!"

Donnie did not heed his words, his anger still powering his actions as he continued to brush the sand out of his eyes.

At the first large tree she came to, Snow scampered up the very large oak within the confines of the village. She was an avid tree climber, had been since she was a little girl. Climbing trees was one of her favorite past times, as was picking flowers, sewing and cooking. She was glad she still had it in her, as she had not climbed for a while since her father had died. Safely away from the others, she broke down, burying her face in her hands. She wished her father were here now to save her. Why not? It was her dream, why couldn't she wish him to be here. She wished very hard, wished him into the very tree she was sitting. But he wasn't there. When was this dream to be over? She even pinched herself to try to awake, but to no avail. She could hear the others down below. They were at the foot of the tree shouting up at her.

"Snow!" said Kate. "Please come down!"

Kristen added, "Yeah, we won't let that Donnie get you! We'll kill him first!"

Kate looked at Kristen, who just shrugged.

"Well, don't put off fer tomorrow what ya can do today!" came Donnie's voice regarding Kristen's remark.

Kristen glared at him, where Jill reminded them, "All right. Look, fight later. Let's get her down from there!"

Donnie started up the tree, "Not a problem."

Snow gasped and grabbed a nearby branch, ripping it from its trunk and hurling it at Donnie, hitting him in the arm.

"Oh, that's it, little missy. Just wait till we get ya down from..."

"Donnie, stop it! Just go. We'll get her down. Haven't you done enough?" Kate pulled him back down with her hand on his shoulder. "Please let us take care of her. You're just scaring her and you know it!"

Donnie backed down, "Well alright, but this isn't over. There is more to this than meets the eye, and I'm gonna find out what it is!"

Kristen pulled him away from the tree, "Just give it a rest, will ya? Leave her alone."

Donnie muttered under his breath as he headed back to the Willows.

"Please come down, Snow. Donnie's a friend of mine. I won't let 'im 'urt ya", pleaded Stevie as Rein and Mitch joined the band at the bottom of the oak.

"Some friend!" Snow sobbed. "With a friend like that, I would just as soon befriend a gypsy!"

Rein stifled a giggle at her statement as he caught a glimpse of her skirt up in the tree. To his disappointment, all his vision caught were the large white bloomers under her tattered dress.

"Please Snow, come on down. We won't let him near you again. I promise." Kate's voice was soothing and Snow wanted so desperately to make friends in this village.

"You do promise?" She sniffled, almost too quietly for the others to hear.

"Yes, we do," promised Kate.

Snow began to make her way down the tree. Upon approaching the bottom, she stepped on one of the branches, and it gave way. Snow gasped and fell the remaining five feet or so and was caught by Mitch in mid-air. Their eyes met for a few seconds before Stevie helped Snow down to the ground and out of Mitch's arms, not even seeming to notice the moment between them. Rein, on the other hand, did notice.

The girls took Snow back to their cabin to help her clean up and put some ice on her head, which had begun to throb once again. After much argument, Stevie finally stopped insisting he tag along. They all went ahead and planned dinner for that evening so Snow's entire story could be told. Kristen just hoped that Snow would tell it without the aid of Stevie. And this time, she would bring her notepad. Kate promised Snow to keep Donnie at a safe distance. As Mitch pondered what meal he could prepare that would prove extra special, he glanced in the direction that the women went. To his surprise, he found Snow glancing back at him as well.

Chapter 2
"Breakfast at Whispering Willows"

The villagers had dinner that evening in the main hut, as they did every evening. The main hut was the largest of the cabins with a large kitchen and outside store room, a dining room and a living area large enough for all of the residents, plus an extra bedroom for guests or for emergencies.

Rein never took his attention away from Donnie's scowl as Snow was telling her story at dinner that evening. He just wanted to be sure there was no repeat of that afternoon's performance. Thankfully for Kristen and the others, Stevie allowed Snow to tell her own story as he was too busy feeding his face with the exceptionally delicious supper Mitch had cooked for the occasion. When asked what it was called, he replied that it was a new recipe he invented called "Snow Surprise" and smiled at her as he said it. Snow blushed heavily. They exchanged occasional glances during dinner, which was also noticed by Rein in between his glances at Donnie.

As Snow described her kingdom, its servants, and her childhood with her mother's death so long ago, she spoke of her favorite hobbies like picking the forest flowers and climbing trees. Her father had even built her a tree house when she was little. She came to tears as she spoke of her father and how close they were. Her 'little princess' was what he called her. Pausing for a moment, Kristen handed her a tissue to wipe her tears. "I'm sorry," Snow apologized for being so weepy.

Kate offered, "You have nothing to be sorry for. You are still in mourning. We understand. It's only been a year."

Ivan pondered how much she reminded him of the women of his time. She really was from his time when he thought about it. They shared similar values, opinions, and memories of what home was like. Duncan, Roger and Bart had similar views as well ... all coming to the Willows from various time periods.

The innocence of this young beauty intrigued Mitch, as he continued to clear the dishes, catching her words here and there. Finally, he decided to finish the dishes later and sat to listen to the conversation.

As the topics led to the subject of chores, Snow's ears perked up. "I can do many chores. I am not a stranger to housework. I can cook and clean and tend to animals. I can clean your cottages spic and span! I can sew my own clothes and I also do mending. I know I need to earn my keep here. May I please stay? I can no longer return home." At the thought, she lowered her eyes in remembering her fate, and the pout returned to her lips.

Even though Rein didn't like to see her sad, this pout of Snow's enticed him every time. He had to keep his thoughts from wandering. And of course, he had to keep an eye on Donnie.

"Of course you can stay." There was a cheer from Stevie as Kristen continued, "We don't want you wandering about the woods," she offered.

"Especially at night," added Kate with a quick glance at Donnie, thinking about the dangers of the woods at night.

The Whispering Willows at night. This was a subject that made all of the villagers fearful. There was a magical, an evil force that would come over the Willows woods at night. It was the reason no one had ever left the Willows. This was just another mystery about the village, along with the 'look-alike' men and the mysterious way all of the residents suddenly 'appear' into the village.

"Yeah, that's the BIG thing. You must NEVER go into the woods at night. So if you decide you 'ave to go pick yer flowers or climb a tree or whatever, you must always be back before dark," warned Donnie sternly.

At his words, Snow's eyes became even larger as she was now always startled at the sound of the barbarian's voice. She reminded herself to never call him that out loud to anyone in the village. However, the title for him would always stick in her head.

As she glanced across the room, she noticed Mitch now sitting with them. Remembering that just a few moments ago, she saw him clearing dishes, "Mitch, would you like some help in washing the dishes? I could start earning my keep right now." She smiled at him.

Mitch would have loved nothing more than to have Snow help him in the kitchen, just the two of them. But he didn't want to ask her to help him with the dishes. He wished she could just sit and talk to him, and he could do the dishes on his own.

Rein quickly offered, "No, I'm sure you are tired from a long day and need your rest. You don't need to be doing any chores tonight." He didn't like the thought of Mitch and Snow alone in the kitchen.

Jill then added, "Yes, you should get some rest. You can stay with me if you like."

Snow was delighted, "Thank you Jill. I so appreciate your hospitality, all of you."

The next morning, Stevie showed up to Jill's cabin before breakfast to take Snow on a tour of the village. Snow had been up even before sunup using the material Jill offered her to sew some new clothes. She managed to alter her white bloomers with some extra material at the top and sides into a pair of 'riding pants' at Jill's suggestion. She had also offered Snow her pick from an assortment of the most lovely shoes. She found a pair that fit perfectly. What were the odds?

Part of the magic of the Willows were the 'magic crates' that would mysteriously show up in the woods with an assortment of supplies, clothes, and other odds and ends. The villagers called them gifts from the 'Willows Fairy'. It was almost as if 'she' would know who was coming to the village next, as the items in the crates would fit the next newcomer perfectly.

The first stop on their tour was the stable. Stevie thought this to be appropriate, since Snow had made herself a pair of riding pants. Even though he hadn't asked permission, he didn't see any harm in going riding with Snow that morning. After all, she was a guest and he wanted to be hospitable. Snow loved horses. She remembered back home to her horse, Sal. She was a beautiful black mare given to her by her father when she was only of eight years. Oh, I mustn't think of sad things, thought Snow as she shook away the memory.

This dream had gotten better since yesterday, although she did think it odd that she had awoken in the village this morning and not in her own bed like she had thought. Well, I guess this dream is going to last a bit longer, Snow decided as she effortlessly mounted the brown mare, and she and Stevie rode about the Willows. For the structures in the village, Stevie showed her all of the villagers' different cabins, along with the chapel, library, jail, mill, surgery and woodshop. For the farming and the animals, which was her favorite part, he showed her the chicken coop, orchards, and fields where they gathered crops, and the main pathway to the clearing where Mitch always picked berries.

They again approached Roger and Murray building the rabbit pen, this time joined by Ivan and Rein.

"Aye, mates!" cried a cheery Stevie.

"Hey, Stevie. Looks like you keep real good company, there." Murray was referring to Snow.

Rein smiled at her and she smiled back, as she petted her mare. Once again, Rein had to catch his thoughts from wandering as he felt a strong sense of jealousy for her horse. Shaking off the thought, he considered himself being childish and continued with his work.

Stevie told Snow, "We're workin' on buildin' a pen 'ere for the rabbits, like we got for the chickens." And then the idea struck him like a lightning bolt as his face lit up. He had to come back and talk to the guys later when Snow wasn't around. "Come on, then. Let's go an' see how long 'fore breakfast. I think Mitch was fixin' up a special welcome breakfast for ya."

Snow asked, "Does Mitch do all of the cooking here?"

Stevie thought for a second, "Well, yeah. I s'pose he does ... mostly, anyway. And Jill cooks, too sometimes."

They rode up to the rear of the kitchen in the main cabin where Mitch was shaking out some towels outside. He stopped and smiled as he saw them.

"Aye, Mitch." Stevie helped Snow down from her horse. "I wondered if you might could show Snow around the kitchen? I have to go check on something."

"Are you leaving?" she asked as he got back on his horse.

"I'll be right back. Just have t' do somethin'."

Mitch smiled. "Don't worry about a thing, Stevie. She won't even notice you're gone." He turned to Snow, "Would you like a tour of the, uh, kitchen?" and he chuckled.

"Yes, thank you. It will go nicely along with the tour Stevie gave me of the village this morning."

He showed her where all of the ingredients and supplies were kept and how the dishes were stored. They swapped cooking stories and versions of recipes of pies and pastries. "I was in fact going to make a pie for this evening of the berries I picked yesterday in our very own berry patch." Mitch picked up a basket of berries and set it down in front of her. "Please try one, they're delicious."

Just as he reached to pick a berry for her out of the basket, Snow reached in to get one and he incidentally grabbed her hand. How soft her skin was, Mitch thought. And how delicate her hands were, just as lovely as their owner. In fact, he couldn't imagine these hands ever doing housework, or any type of chore, for that matter. He held her hand for a moment and then realized, "Oh, I'm sorry. Here..." He let her hand go and gave her a handful of berries. Nervously, he tried to recover, "Delicious, aren't they?"

She smiled. "Yes, very," Snow also hinted a nervousness in her voice. As she offered to help with breakfast, she thought to herself that maybe she would rather not wake from this dream after all.

"Hey, good job everyone," said Murray as the men looked down at their work. They had completed the rabbit pen in record time.

"'ello, again!" yelled Stevie as he rode up on his horse and jumped down.

"Hey, Stevie," Ivan greeted him with a smile, still quite happy about the finished pen.

"Guys, I 'ad this great idea, and I wondered if'n you could 'elp me wit it."

"What is it, Stevie?" inquired Roger with a hint of fear.

"I 'ad this idea for Snow, a place for 'er to stay, ya know. I thought, wha' 'bout a treehouse!!"

The men looked at each other with dread.

Stevie continued, "Ya know, ya remember at dinner last night when she talked 'bout her treehouse being her favorite place to go?"

Murray approached him, "But Stevie, I don't think she would actually want to LIVE in a treehouse. Do you?"

Stevie lit up with excitement, "Why sure! Why not? She used to love it and she still loves to climb trees, ya know."

Ivan offered, "Well, alright. We can ask her about it at break-fast".

Stevie shook his head, "No, it 'as to be a surprise, ya know. She can't know nothin' 'bout it, OK? I'm gonna go tell the girls, they'll love this. See ya!"

Once Stevie was out of earshot, Murray ran his hands through his hair, "What are we going to do with him? Does he have any idea how hard a treehouse would be to build and then hoist into a tree?"

"I'm sure he doesn't," offered Roger.

A treehouse! What a wonderful idea, thought the girls as they whispered amongst themselves. Whether Snow decided to live in it or not, the girls decided that a treehouse would make the perfect escape. What better location to have a romantic rendezvous, for example, thought Kate. Kristen was thinking how much closer the treehouse would be than the woods to be by herself for a change, or NOT by herself, perhaps. Jill thought it would make a perfect place to read a book uninterrupted.

Stevie was concerned that the other men wouldn't help him. "But I dunno that the guys thought it to be such a great idea, ya know. I dunno 'ow 'ard a treehouse is to build." He knew he could never build one by himself... not one that would actually hold the weight of someone, anyway.

"Don't you worry your cute little head about a thing, Stevie, " began Jill, "They'll build it. Heck, if Snow takes to it, we may even get them to build a spare one just for recreation." She looked at Kate, who then winked back at Jill.

Breakfast was delicious as usual. There was no talk about the treehouse in Snow's presence, but the news had gotten around. The men seemed a little grouchier than usual to have given in to the request of Stevie and the girls. Jill actually hoped that Snow would hate the thing, so that they wouldn't have to wait for the men to build another one.

Mitch reminded Donnie that it was his turn to do the dishes.
"Wha'?"
Mitch nodded his head.
"That's right, Donnie. I remember" Kate said as she giggled.
"Why can't the new 'PRINCESS' get the dishes? She needs to earn her keep around here, anyway. Great, now we 'ave a new 'Your Majesty' to tend to," as Donnie gave Kate a look that she gave right back to him.

Jill must have seen the wide-eyed expression on Snow's face at the sound of the 'barbarian's' voice discussing her, as she gently put her hand on Snow's shoulder. "Don't pay him any attention. He's just grumpy."

Stevie's face lit up and he sprung from the table, "Aye, Grumpy!" Stevie pointed at Eddy, "And he's Sleepy! And over there is Doc and Bashful!"

"And you're Dopey!!" Donnie cut in.

There was hysterical laughter around the room. Snow smiled at their joy, but hadn't a clue as to what was so funny. "Did I miss something?" she inquired, which made the room break into hysterics all the more.

"No, you didn't miss a thing, dear," offered Kate. "Let's take a walk. Come on, girls. Let's all of us have some quality 'girl talk'." The women excused themselves and started on a hike through the woods.

The women shared with Snow their experiences here in the village and in turn told how each one happened upon the Willows. They talked about their attractions to the male members of the village, as well as who they were NOT attracted to.

When they asked Snow if she thought her newfound companions attractive, she blushed, "Oh well, yes I would, I guess. But I cannot consider an alliance with someone who is not of royal blood. It is our decree."

Kristen frowned, "But Snow, you aren't in your kingdom here. You are no longer bound by any decree. You are free to do as you wish here."

Snow added, "But it is what my father would have wanted. So it appears that I am out of luck. The only one of royalty here is not someone that I would ever choose to form an alliance with."

Kristen offered, "You mean Eddy?"

Snow was puzzled, "No the barbar ... I mean that Donnie fellow. Yesterday he said he was the King of England."

The three women burst into a symphony of hysterical laughter.

Jill offered, "Oh, goodness we have had two good laughs today. We are so glad you came, Snow!"

Kate was on the ground, tears streaming down her face. She couldn't even speak, she was laughing so hard.

Kristen turned back to the puzzled young girl, "No, Snow. He isn't the King of England. That was just a statement of sorts."

Snow looked somewhat relieved, and then inquired, "Then what were you saying about Eddy?"

Kate got up still giggling, "Oh, no, not Eddy. You don't want Eddy."

Jill added, "No, Eddy is, how shall I put this, not in the 'wife seeking' mode at the moment. I'll just put it that way."

'Eddy' referred to Edward II to be specific, who came to the Willows from the fourteenth century, and preferred men over women ... one in particular who did not enter the Willows with him.

Snow looked somewhat disappointed. "Oh, well. No never-mind. I should be waking up from this dream any moment any-how. So I guess it doesn't matter."

Kristen frowned, "What do you mean by that? Are you say-ing you think this is all a dream?"

"Of course, " Snow replied. "I know these things couldn't possibly happen. My stepmother would never try to kill me, I could not possibly fall through a hole in the woods THAT big, and there is no possible way that a village like this really exists where all of the men look the same."

The other women laughed again.

Snow continued, "But the strangest part about it is that they all look exactly like the prince I keep dreaming about, which is what made me realize this is all just a dream."

Jill retorted, "Well, maybe we're all having the same dream then. I wouldn't rule it out."

Kristen thought for a second, "Wait a minute, did you just say that all the men look just like someone in your dreams?"

Snow nodded, "Yes. I dream about a handsome prince all the time, one that someday will carry me away to his kingdom."

Jill leaned in to Kate, "Good thing Donnie isn't here."

Kate nodded in agreement.

Snow was still puzzled by the whole situation.

Kristen tried to reassure her, "Snow, I assure you, you are not dreaming. Believe me, we all had the same thought, that this whole thing was a dream and we would wake up in our own bed at any given moment. Well, it took a while, but we finally were able to come to the realization that it just isn't so. We are really here. And you are welcome to stay as long as you like."

Snow didn't know what to think about it all. Should she believe these women? They seemed to be genuinely concerned for her. She wanted to trust them, she really did.

Jill added, "Oh and about your stepmother, forget her! Believe me when I tell you that the whole reason behind that plot was because she was jealous of you, Snow! You were prettier than she was and the whole kingdom favored you over her, and she knew it."

Snow was fighting back tears, "But how do you know that?"

Kate offered, "Jill has special insight into things sometimes, dear. She is telling the truth, you can trust her words. Everything is going to be OK."

Jill giggled, "Yes, and of course we all couldn't help but notice that Stevie has a mad crush on you."

Snow looked surprised, "Stevie?"

Kate added, "Oh yes, no way around it!"

Snow sniffled, "Well, I think Stevie is really nice and will probably make a good friend but he isn't..."

"Oh, please don't say he isn't royalty, " Kristen interrupted. "That's what you were going to say, wasn't it?"

Snow nodded.

"Well, don't you worry your pretty little head, these men are all 'princes' of a sort, and I would think many of them would fancy you."

Jill smiled, "Yes, I seem to recall Mitch looking in your direction an awful lot this morning."

Kate teased back, "Ah, you noticed that too, Jill?"

Kristen turned to go, "Well, let's head on back and see what the fellows are up to. We gotta make sure they aren't makin' any trouble, ya know."

Kate and Jill laughed. Snow smiled and thought that if this were to not be a dream, that she may be able to be happy here.

However, as she remembered the words of her new friends, she couldn't help but think back on her kingdom's decree.

Chapter 3
"The 24-Carrot Dance"

Isn't this a lovely afternoon, thought Snow? Although she appreciated Stevie's company, she didn't have the heart to tell him that the book he was reading to her was quite appalling in her eyes, a brutal story that she found no interest in. She was actually thankful to the barbarian himself for dragging Stevie away to talk about some kind of wood structure, or something like that. It allowed her the chance to drift into her thoughts, taking in all of this newfound excitement and pondering the events of the past two days. What of this 'mad crush' the girls mentioned that Stevie had on her? Could it be true? And what about Mitch? She really enjoyed his company as well, and they have so many things in common. She wasn't sure what she felt about them, any of them. She didn't want to know, didn't want to allow herself to feel more than a friendship for any one of these men. She couldn't betray her decree, betray her father. She loved her father.

Yet still, she felt ... what was that? Snow heard a tiny little chirping noise. Where was it coming from? She lowered her head, lower, lower still. It was coming from somewhere on the ground. There, in that pile, a patch of blue. It moved! As she drew closer she could see it. It was a tiny bird. A baby blue jay!

"Have you lost your mamma and papa?" She looked all around in the trees and in the air, but saw no signs of any other blue jays. "I've lost my mamma and papa, too." She knelt down and gently scooped up the baby. "I'll take care of you."

Wait, what was that? Another noise? She covered the bird

with her other hand and walked in the direction of the sound. This sound was deeper and was getting louder and louder with each step. Peering from behind a tree, she saw it. Lying in the distance was a horse, a mare. She sounded hurt. Snow approached the mare and saw that she was about to give birth! Tending to horses, she had seen this before.

She knew she needed to get help. "Goodness, I'll be right back. Just hang on!!" Still holding the bird, she ran back to the village. She recalled that Kate told her of the mare that had run away when Bart accidentally forgot to properly lock the stable. This had to be the one.

She found most of the men discussing a project by a large pile of wood. Thinking that Bart would most probably like to redeem himself for his mistake, she called to him and he rushed over accompanied by Stevie upon seeing Snow.

"Bart, that mare that escaped the other day is about to give birth in the woods! Come quickly!"

"Good Lord! Ivan, Roger come here!" The two men approached. Bart continued, "Snow says that escaped mare is about to give birth in the woods. We need to hurry!"

The men gathered some supplies and darted into the woods. Stevie, still standing with Snow glanced at her hands with curiosity, "Wha' ya got there, Snow?"

"Shhhh", hushed Snow. "Come and I will show you."

Snow headed back for Jill's cabin with Stevie following behind. Snow sat on the bed. "Sit," she said "and then be careful." Between them, she set the delicate little bird on the bed.

Stevie's face lit up, "Aye, it's a bird!"

"Yes, it's a baby blue jay. Be very gentle with him."

Stevie attempted to pet the bird, but then decided not to.

Snow smiled, "I named him Tweety"

Stevie laughed, "Aye! And what about Sylvester?"

Snow was puzzled, "What?"

"Oh, I forgot that ya don't ... oh nevermind. He's a cute bird, there Snow."

"What's this?" came Jill's voice in the doorway.

"What are you two doing on the bed?" joked Kate.

Snow was startled, "Oh Jill, Kate, you gave me such a shock!"

"Why's that? Ya weren't doing anything that ya weren't supposed to, were ya?" Jill winked. "Hey, whatcha got there?" she inquired.

Stevie whispered as though he had to be quiet around the bird, "It's a baby blue jay. Snow found it in the woods."

Snow said back to Stevie, "It's OK Stevie, you don't have to whisper. The poor thing didn't seem to have any parents, so I adopted him."

Kate cooed, "Oh, well isn't he cute?"

Snow smiled. "Yes, I named him Tweety."

Jill giggled, "So where's Sylvester?"

Snow frowned at hearing that name again, "Who is Sylvester? Everyone seems to know but me."

Jill looked at Stevie who just shrugged. "Sorry, Snow. There is a famous cartoon duo name Sylvester and Tweety."

"Cartoon?" inquired Snow.

Kate smiled as she watched Snow bond with the little bird. Tweety didn't even seem frightened anymore.

You really seem to have a motherly touch, there" Kate offered.

Snow smiled, then thought back to what little she remembered of her mother.

"I'm sorry, Snow. I didn't mean to make you sad" Kate said, mentally scolding herself for bringing up the thought.

"No, that's alright. I like to think about her. I was so young when she died. Funny, my father remarried to try and help me, not hurt me. Margurite wasn't even his first choice as my stepmother, she was his third. He was truly in love with Cynthia. But my father was shy and not fast enough in proposing, so alas she accepted a proposal from the King of Hughes, thinking that my father would never ask. But she was wonderful. She was kind and we had so much in common. She lost her mother at an early age, too. Her father remarried a woman with two daughters. After his death, they treated her just horribly. They wouldn't even call her by her real name. Instead they called her..."

"Cinderella!" Jill interrupted.

Snow's eyes widened, "Yes, how did you know that?"

Jill smiled, "I had a vision."

Kate giggled.

"What about his second choice?" Jill inquired. "You said your stepmother was his third."

Snow added, "Yes, he would have proposed to a princess over near Euphrania, but rumor had it that they were all asleep, the entire town! It was very odd."

Jill and Kate just looked at each other.

"That's it girl, just one more push." soothed Ivan as he stroked the mare's mane.

"I've got him!" cried Bart as he pulled the remainder of the colt's legs free. "It's a boy!!"

"Hooray" cried the others who had joined the birth in the woods when they heard the news.

After the birth, the mare practically sprung to her feet.

"Thank God it was an easy birth for her. She could just have easily been held up for days. I've seen it happen too many times," suggested Ivan. "Looks like you've redeemed yourself, there Bart."

Bart carefully scooped up the colt in a blanket. The group headed back to the village.

The blossoms on the trees are so lovely, not something you see every day, thought Snow as she walked through the Whispering Willows orchard.

Just then she saw Mitch. "Mitch, hello! Fancy meeting you here!"

Seeing Snow thrilled Mitch to no end. "Snow, what a most pleasant surprise. What are you doing in the orchard?"

She trotted over to the tree he was picking from, "Oh, I just wanted to see what all types of fruit the village had to choose from. What kinds of pies you can make, things like that. Looks like I picked a perfect time. You are here to show me."

Mitch took her hand to lead her around the orchard, "Very true. Here we have peach, plum, and apricot trees for the warmer seasons. And over there we have the apple and orange trees for the cooler seasons."

"What were you picking just now?" Snow inquired.

"Ah, I was choosing the most perfect peaches to bake a pie for a very special someone."

Snow bit her lip, "Can I help you pick a peach for this special someone?"

Mitch smiled and paused to think it funny that this little 'peach' would be picking a peach for herself. "Of course, my lady. Be my guest, but be careful."

Snow climbed the ladder as Mitch held onto it. She glanced around the tree, looking for the best peach. Then she saw it ... the most perfect plump peach. She reached ... argh! Just out of her reach. She elevated onto her toes on the ladder.

"Careful dear," warned Mitch once again.

She grabbed a branch above her for support and pulled herself up ever so slightly to just touch the peach with her fingertips. Snap! The branch she held onto for support broke, sending her backwards off of the ladder. Thump! An all too familiar scene for Snow, as once again she found herself in Mitch's arms after falling out of a tree. Their eyes met again, their noses almost touching. Snow found herself struggling with her feelings again, specifically her feelings for Mitch. One cannot just stifle one's feelings for someone just like that. However, she made a conscious effort to brush them away.

This is such a beautiful and precious girl, thought Mitch. She is so innocent and trusting, that he dared not kiss her, although he wanted to. "Dejavu! We have to stop meeting like this, eh?" joked Mitch as he set her down gently.

"I'm so sorry I'm such a clutz," Snow offered.

"Nonsense," Mitch assured her. "Happens all the time around here. I have had more falls out of orchard trees than I can count. Had my share of bumps and bruises, too. But I have enough peaches here I think. Come on. Let's get back to the village. We don't want to be late for dinner. Jill is cooking tonight. Think I'll enjoy the break. I'll make you a cuppa. Sound good?"

Snow nodded. She didn't quite understand the wording, 'cuppa', but coming from a friend like Mitch, it must be a good thing.

"Where is she?" inquired Stevie.

"If I didn't know five minutes ago Stevie, why would I know now?" retorted Kate.

Then seeing his sad expression, "Look Stevie, I'm sure she'll be here any minute. Why don't you go into the kitchen and see if Jill needs a hand with dinner, eh?"

Stevie smiled and nodded and dashed into the kitchen.

Kristen giggled, "I think he's hooked! I also think he's starting to drive Snow crazy!"

Kate looked at her, "You really think so?"

"Well I do," Rein added. "I think he is definitely driving her mad. And if I have anything to say about it, tonight she's getting a break from him for a change."

Kate and Kristen exchanged raised eyebrow looks at Rein's statement. Just then, the door to the main cabin opened and Mitch and Snow entered with a basket of peaches.

"Well, it's about time!" Kate scolded in jest.

"Yeah, I think Stevie was about to send out a search party for you ... namely himself. He's in the kitchen if you'd like to announce your presence and save his sanity," Kristen offered as she eyed the basket of peaches. "Nice bushel there, Mitch," she added.

Snow entered the kitchen to find Stevie drying a cooking pan. "Hey, heard you were looking for me, Stevie."

"Snow!" Stevie dropped the pan and it crashed to the floor loudly. He ran over to Snow and hugged her tightly. "I was worried about ya. I didn't know where ya was," he sighed.

"I was fine Stevie," Snow coughed, finding it difficult to talk within such a bear hug. "I was picking peaches with Mitch in the orchard."

Mitch overheard as he passed through with the peaches, "Yes, Stevie. You shouldn't worry. Snow will always be well cared for around here."

Jill offered, "Yes, as will the rest of us girls. Right Mitch?" Jill winked at him.

"Right, Jill." And he winked back.

Stevie showed concern, "Well, I worry 'bout them woods and all. Didn't want you to get sucked into 'nother hole or nothin'."

Snow smiled, "Well, that is very sweet of you Stevie, and I do appreciate your concern for my well-being. Jill, do you need a hand here in the kitchen?"

"No, but thanks. If Stevie here'll stop dropping pans and making enough noise ta wake the dead, I think he'll be able ta help me enough," as Jill looked at Stevie who took the hint and picked up the pan he dropped.

Snow entered back into the dining room.

"Man, what was all the clattering in there?" inquired Kristen.

Snow smiled, "Oh, Stevie was just a little too glad to see me and dropped his pan to rush over and make sure I was alright ... harmless act."

"But annoying nonetheless," Rein said under his breath where only Kate and Nicholas could hear him.
Nicholas, a scholar and explorer of Africa from the early twentieth century, coughed to stifle a laugh.

Dinner was delicious as usual. Jill fixed a wonderful cajun dish with rice and catfish from the river. Jill was from New Orleans, near the bayou and cajun as you get. Raised in a voodoo family, she was familiar with the customs, but wasn't practicing, herself.

"This is delicious, Jill. Did you catch the fish at the usual spot in the river? asked Kristen.

Finishing the bite in her mouth, Jill offered "Actually I can't take credit for the catfish. That was Eddy's doing."

Edward smiled, "Yes, I'm quite fond of fishing, actually. I was pleasantly surprised to discover that we have some nice breeds of catfish down in the river. I find it very relaxing to fish, personally."

Snow made a mental note of this.

After dinner, it was Stevie's turn to do the dishes, much to Rein's delight as he asked Snow if she would like to go visit the newborn colt in the stable.

"Oh yes!" she squealed. She hadn't seen the newest edition to Whispering Willows as of yet and wanted to very much.

Rein stopped at the door and looked at Nicholas

"It's all set up," Nicholas said.

Rein patted him on the shoulder, "Thanks, Nicholas."

The explorer grinned, "No problem, but you owe me BIG for this one!"

Rein slowly opened the barn door to let the both of them in and then carefully closed the door behind them. He didn't want to wake the colt if he was sleeping.

"Oh, he is so precious!" Snow cooed as she saw the little colt curled up in the hay. He wasn't sleeping, but looked like he would be at any moment. "He is such a beautiful golden color." Snow added.

Rein smiled, "Jill decided on a name for him. She said since he is such a nice golden color and because horses love carrots, she named him '24-Carrots'. They judge the quality of gold in a measurement called 'carats', now." After a few moments of gazing at the little fellow, Rein asked, "Do you like dancing, Snow?"

Snow's face lit up, "I love dancing! However, I haven't danced in what seems like ages."

Rein offered his arm, "Then shall we?" As Snow took his arm he led her to an open section of the barn, he said, "Here, I want to show you something."

He went over to a bail of hay that had a small black box sitting on top of it. The box was strange looking to Snow, as she had never seen anything like it before. Rein had asked Nicholas to set this up for him just before dinner. A few weeks ago, the men in the village found a crate with this box among its contents. Donnie told Rein it was something called a 'CD player'. Donnie complained that the CD that came with the player contained only waltz music and then mentioned that he hoped the next crate they found had something in it called 'rock and roll', whatever that was. Rein, however, found the CD to be perfect music for dancing. After Rein pushed a few buttons on the odd contraption, out of it began to play the most beautiful music Snow had ever heard.

She gasped, "Rein, is that a magical box? How can a box so small hold so many people playing instruments of that sort? I've never heard music of that kind."

Rein smiled, "Yes, we found this little gem in the village a little while back. It is actually quite simple to operate. Shall we?" Rein took her hand in the air and put his other hand on her waist and she rested hers on his shoulder.

Rein was an excellent dancer, Snow thought. This 'waltz' music was very enjoyable. After some time of various chit chat and comments on the music, there started to play a rather slow piece that placed the two of them at an almost stand still of a dance pace. Rein hadn't been able to take his eyes off of her the entire evening. She had made a new dress that afternoon of a soft light blue material that swished around her ankles as she walked. The blue in her dress brought out the blue in her eyes in the most astounding way, thought Rein, that he couldn't help but gaze into them. At which point, Snow found herself gazing back. What was going on here, Snow thought? What am I doing? She feared now that she was leading this gentleman on in such a way that was just not right. Then why did she feel the way she did? What was it about his romantic nature and sincere attentiveness that attracted her so? She felt drawn as though she were physically unable to retract her gaze from his. It's true ... she thought that Stevie was a sweetheart, and Mitch was so kind and giving, but Rein had something about him. What was it? It was a special charm that he possessed, in that he knew how a girl wanted to be looked at, or talked to in a certain way...like he brought just the right romantic spark to a conversation. How was that? She had no experience in such things, yet felt something extra special in being in such a romantic presence.

Yet, there was something she couldn't quite put her finger on, something else going on. Was there another motive in having her in his company, maybe? No, Rein was quite the gentleman and Snow just couldn't imagine otherwise. He wasn't like some of those palace guards that she would avoid walking past due to the strange way they stared at her, almost seeming to undress her with their eyes. No, no, no! That was not what this was. Not at all! Rein was not like that, so what was it then? She didn't quite know the answer.

Then as she compared her visits with Mitch in relation to her talks with Rein, her thoughts were interrupted as Rein leaned in to kiss her. What do I do now, she thought? Do I stop him? Before she could answer her own question, Rein was softly kissing her. It could only barely have been just a few seconds, but seemed like an eternity as her thoughts screamed through her head. Why is he kissing me? Does this mean he is wanting to be more than friends? Is this like a mad crush? Why did I kiss him back? Why aren't I stopping him now? What is this I am feeling for this gentleman? Wait, gentleman, but not of royalty! The decree ... DADDY!!!

Snow gasped and pulled away, "I'm sorry. I..."

Rein gave a look of concern and put his hands on her shoulders, "Snow, are you alright? I didn't mean to scare you. I'm sorry."

Snow was terribly nervous, and her head still screaming its thoughts so loudly, she felt she had to raise her own voice slightly to hear herself over them, "No, Rein it isn't you. It's my ... I mean it's me. I was in the wrong, not you. I'm sorry."

Rein touched her cheek, "Snow you did nothing wrong. What's..."

She interrupted, "I'm sorry, I should go now. But thank you very much for bringing me to see 24-Carrots."

Before Rein could say anything else, Snow was out the door. She rushed back to the cabin in a dead sprint.

By the time she reached the porch of her and Jill's cabin, she was sobbing uncontrollably. Luckily, Jill was still out with the others. She dashed over to where she kept her clothes and pulled out her blue lace-up top from her original outfit from home. She carefully unpinned the broach from the top, and held it tightly in her hand as she slid to the floor. This was her family crest, her father's crest. Did she disappoint him tonight? Was he saddened as he looked down at her from heaven? "I'm sorry, Daddy!" she sobbed. "I will not dishonor the family crest, Daddy. I will not dishonor the decree. I won't! I..." She couldn't talk anymore through her sobs as they were too heavy, causing her to gasp for air. She got up and walked over to the little sleeping bird she had befriended and gave a weak smile. "In fact Tweety," she sniffed, "... tomorrow, I shall go fishing."

Chapter 4
"Go Fish"

"Oh, you gals make such a mess!" Snow scolded the chickens as she cleaned the coop. "I'm going to have to get a fresh bucket of water to do the rabbits. My, my!!" As Snow picked up the bucket and turned to leave, something caught her eye over in the corner leaning against the chicken wire. It was a fishing pole and tackle box. It's still here, she thought. She would have assumed that most fishermen start early, but then of course people don't fish every day. Stop being silly Snow, she thought. If not today, there will be other days. Her thoughts drifted to the conversation she had the previous afternoon with Yolanda and Duncan. She enjoyed talking with them. At one point, the subject had rolled over into one's position in society and the like. From there, Snow just couldn't help but ask about their views on royalty.

Duncan was from the mid eighteenth century as a British soldier during the French and Indian war. With him being under the crown's military service during his life, he had much to say on the matter. It was through this topic, that Snow was able to get the answers she needed about Edward. He was from a royal bloodline, and he was the only one in the village that was, at least at this current time. What Snow didn't understand was why all the women in the village, including Yolanda, kept trying to steer her away from him? He seemed like a nice enough gentleman, although she had not yet had an opportunity to get to know him quite yet. What was the problem they saw? She just didn't see it. Why did Jill say that he wasn't in a 'wife seeking' mode? Why did Yolanda agree when I told her what Jill said? Well, at any rate, he would certainly make a better companion than that Donnie fellow, for example. Who wouldn't, she thought?

She returned with the new bucket of water for the rabbit pen. "You guys are so cute! And you aren't nearly as messy as those chickens over there." An especially fluffy white rabbit caught her eye. "Well, hello there! I wonder where they got you from? You look much too pretty to have been fetched out of the woods. You are snowy white!" Snow laughed out loud hearing the unintentional joke she just made. "I will call you Whitie. I would call you Snowy, but I would be afraid that would get confusing to some folks." She giggled and put Whitie back into the pen, then continued with her work.

Upon leaving, something made her stop dead in her tracks. The fishing equipment was gone! How did I miss that? Oh, of course. It must have been when I went to get the water. Well, now is my chance. "Oh yuck! I can't go like this!" Snow looked down at her 'chores outfit' of what the girls call 'jeans' and one of the men's shirts, a very large one at that. "I have chicken stuff all over me!" Remembering back to last night when she couldn't sleep, she finished a dress in the loveliest pink silken material. That would be perfect.

"Wow! That's beautiful, Snow. Where are you going all dressed up this morning?" inquired Jill as she scanned the lovely pink dress.

"Um, nowhere. I got chicken goop on my chores outfit."

Jill made a sour face at the thought, "Yuck. Sorry they had you doing that so soon."

Snow smiled, "That's OK. I love animals. I think I'll go check on 24-Carrots, speaking of animals."

Why not, she thought. He is such a cute little thing, and it's on the way to the river. As she approached, she caught a glimpse of Rein going into the barn, apparently to check on the colt as well. Snow stopped. Oh dear, she thought. I really can't run into him again, especially in the barn where they kissed the previous night. She hoped he wasn't angry with her for leaving so suddenly. She didn't want to hurt him. She didn't know how he felt about her. But what frightened her more was that she didn't know what she felt about him.

Although he had returned the CD player, he could still hear the melody of the waltz as he relived the dance with Snow in his thoughts. She was so lovely, Rein thought. She still is lovely, of course, but it was that innocent nature of hers that had really taken him. Her doe-eyed expression, her full lips that he had seen pout so often that first day she was here. It seemed that she had grown up since then. That scared young girl was now open and friendly with everyone, and in such a short time. She didn't even seem as afraid of Donnie as she was at first. He hoped he hadn't frightened her last night. "Blasted, what was I thinking! Stop rushing things Partridge!" He spoke out loud and awakened the sleeping colt. "Oh, I'm sorry 24-Carrots. I didn't mean to be so loud. I should just keep my thoughts to myself, eh?" He reached down and petted the colt, who quickly went back to sleep.

As she traveled the path to the river, she grew nervous with each passing tree. What am I doing, Snow thought? I don't know this man at all. But that is why I'm doing this, right? To get to know him better? What things will I say? 'Here I am! Whacha doing?' just didn't seem like the right way to approach the situation. He will want to know why I'm here. Oh dear. Why am I here? Oh my, I have to think of something. Mmmm. Well, I haven't seen the river yet and decided to seek it out. I guess that would work. I'm always curious about nature, so that wouldn't be a lie. OK, got that part down. What things will I say? Should I ask about his kingdom? His family? She promised herself not to stay long. This man will be fishing and enjoying his time alone. Don't bother him and make him hate you, Snow! She wished she had one of those contraptions for her wrist that the others called a 'watch' so she could keep the time of her visit.

She could hear the babbling of the brook as she grew closer. With each step her heart pounded louder. She came to a clearing. There! Sitting on a large rock holding the fishing pole, of course, was the prince ... I mean was Edward ... or is it Eddy? She must remember to NOT call him 'prince'. That was just unnatural in this village, even though perfectly acceptable and expected in her kingdom. What was it Yolanda once said? 'We're not in Kansas anymore, Toto'? Wherever Kansas is, and whoever Toto is. But she wasn't too fond of calling him 'Eddy'. She much preferred Edward. It sounded more proper and more like a name she was used to. But what if he likes 'Eddy' better? Sakes, Snow you are making this so difficult. You always do that. Stop it! OK, deep breath ... not too loud, though. Alright, here goes.

"Oh, Edward, hello. I wasn't expecting to find you here." She held her breath just waiting on the lightning bolt to strike her down for such a blatant lie.

"Snow, greetings. How are you this beautiful morning?"

Snow smiled, "Very well, thank you." She hoped against hope that there wasn't a crack in her voice that would give him any indication of how nervous she was. She thought back to the talks she used to overhear at home. She would softly creep down the large staircase and stand just within earshot of her father and the other monarchs. They would speak about the arranged marriages of their sons and daughters. Snow was always amazed at the fact that unions would be planned for people that had never even met. She remembered the sick feeling in her stomach when she would think that she would ever unite with someone she had never met. Well, it wouldn't be happening this time, she thought.

"Are they biting much?" Snow asked politely. Luckily for her, she had been fishing one time with a noble that was a good friend of her father's. She was able to catch some of the fishing terminology from him. She just hoped she remembered it correctly.

"Ah, not really today. But I guess since we just had fish last night, we wouldn't really be needing any more for a little while. I just find it relaxing. I can just sit and be one with nature. That sort of thing, you know?"

Snow almost panicked, "Oh, well if you would rather be alone, I ...."

With a laugh, Ed calmed her fears, "No, that's alright. Please stay and sit for a while. I think I have been 'one' long enough this morning."

As Snow smiled and sat next to Edward, a wave of relief passed over Snow almost like cool water flowing over the top of her head. She had felt so warm. Oh, dear, she hoped her face wasn't flustering and turning red as it sometimes does. She took a quick glance into the water at her reflection. Her cheeks were slightly pink, but not too red, thankfully.

"Yes, the water is quite clear, isn't it?" as Ed saw her peering into the water.

"Yes, very." Snow, embarrassed that she had been caught, tried to recover. "So, what are your favorite kinds of fish?" Oh, gosh, did I just say that, thought Snow? What a stupid and childish question. He's going to think you've the brain of a child!

Edward happily began discussing the different types of fish he had seen in the river along with which ones were the easiest and hardest to catch. "My favorite is shellfish, which of course, is only found in the ocean. Before I came to the village, my ... um ... friend and I used to trap different shellfish off of the ocean's coast back home."

A shudder went through Snow when Edward mentioned 'back home'. This is my open door, she thought. "Please tell me more about where you came from, your heritage? I am very curious about other royal houses."

Edward remembered, "Oh yes, I almost forgot, you are of royal blood as well, aren't you? House of White, wasn't it? Well, I'm sure we are probably more lax on such things than in your kingdom, but we may share many things in common."

Upon hearing this, Snow was delighted and soaked in every word as Edward went on about royal customs and history. He was right, in that things were different than where she came from. But nevertheless, Snow found his words fascinating.

As she watched, she of course couldn't help but ponder in her mind the similarities of the men in the village. Edward reminded her of Rein who reminded her of Mitch who reminded her of Stevie and so on. Each one possessed qualities different from the others. Rein had a sense of romanticism that was, by her standards, perfected by trade so to speak. Rein knew how to treat a lady and how one wished to be treated. To Snow, this most probably meant that he had many women in the past, which wasn't the most pleasant thought to Snow. Then there was Mitch. He was so sweet and giving. Women were not new to him either, but she found her opinion of him to be that he was still searching for that certain 'someone', and searching very hard for that matter. She'd heard that he seemed to ask every woman in the village at some point to dinner or tea or something, which was alright, I guess, Snow thought. She liked his company. They both had much in common. He was charming and easy to talk to. She found herself thinking back to the two times Mitch had caught her in midair falling from those two trees and remembered the gaze into his eyes. That gaze they shared that seemed to last a lifetime, even if only for a second. She found herself watching Edward and looking for similarities in him to that of Mitch.

Snow, stop that! This is Edward, Prince Edward ... KING even! He is his own person. Stop looking for someone else. You haven't even gotten to know him yet. He seemed sweet and friendly, and also open to conversation. Many of the others weren't so eager to converse so friendly and freely, like Donnie. Oh, my lands, don't think about Donnie! Moving right along ... Edward. Right, OK. Edward. Well there was something ... different about him that Snow couldn't quite put her finger on. She couldn't say if that were a good thing or a bad thing. Although he was friendly, he was also distant in that he didn't have the same ... what is the word ... affection in his voice when he spoke with Snow as some of the others did, like Mitch. And in his eyes, although friendly, lacked what the other men had shown within each of their gazes, especially, for example, the gazes of Rein or Mitch. And of course, Stevie was a whole different story altogether. He was fun to be around and his attentiveness was very flattering. However, he wasn't used to being in a lady's company for a long period of time, in that, Snow didn't think he quite knew what kinds of activities a lady preferred or subjects to speak on. Plus, Stevie was just plain shy. She thought if he was ever kissed by a woman, he would probably faint dead away ... well almost.

Snow noticed that Edward had one of those wristwatch contraptions. "Oh, do you have the time?"
Looking at his watch, "Yes, it is nearly twelve, by about ten minutes or so. Perhaps we should head back to the village? I'm sure lunch will be ready soon. I can't remember who is cooking today, though."

Snow thought it would be nice to walk back to the village with Edward, but she in no way wanted Kate, or Jill, or Kristen, or even Yolanda to see her walking with him. What an obvious little plight that would be!

"I believe it is Thomas cooking this day."

Edward's eyes rolled, "Oh good Lord. I hope we make it out alive!"

He laughed at his own remarks, but Snow was so distracted with her own thoughts she merely smiled, "Do you mind terribly if I follow along in a few minutes. I just remembered something I need to do."

Edward smiled, but wondered if perhaps the joke he made was not all that funny, "Yes, of course. I will see you at lunch."

What a nice young girl, thought Eddy. She was sweet and her innocence quite refreshing. He thought that she seemed quite lonely. Perhaps she was homesick, and he, being of a royal background, probably reminds her of home. He enjoyed her company and thought she could probably be a good friend. If he could help her 'homesickness' and make her feel more comfortable here in the village, then he was glad to help.

Thomas had received some help, no doubt, from Mitch in his preparation of their lunch, as the luncheon to everyone's surprise was quite good.

Thomas Kelligan came from the late eighteenth century. His wife and son were murdered by a 'madman' of sorts. He tried to save them, but when the madmad came after him, his demise landed him here in the Willows.

The mood in the room was jovial. The weather had been very nice the past few days and seemed to lift everyone's spirits. The biggest topic at lunch was no doubt the Halloween festival, which was suggested by, of course, Jill ... resident 'spiritual specialist'. After a brief explanation on how Halloween is celebrated today, Jill suggested everyone dress up in a costume of sorts. She then offered to help out in any way she could on the costuming.

Snow was also eager to help. In her day, Halloween was referred to as 'All Hallow's Eve' and was considered a day of fear and evildoing. She was glad that things were not that way any longer. It sounded like a fun day in these terms, and she was busy thinking of what she could dress up to be. A bride, maybe? EEEK! Snow, stop it! Stop it right now! Snow scolded herself for the thought. She was glad no one in the room could read her thoughts, especially the men, lest they all run out the door and into the woods screaming!

Stevie was excited about the festival as well, "Donnie, wha' ya gonna dress up as?"

Donnie scowled, "Ow 'bout this. I'll be Donnie, and you can be Stevie, and you can be Ivan, and so on," as he motioned to the others.

Kate gave him 'the look', which this time he did not return. She appeared half disappointed that he didn't.

Duncan added, "In my day, we called these occasions 'masquerades' and everyone wore a mask. You had to guess at who everyone was."

Yolanda squealed and patted his arm, "Oh, what a wonderful

idea, dear! Can we do that for the festival?"

Jill thought for a second, "You know, that may not be a bad idea. But of course, you have to consider that the guys are going to have a huge advantage over us there. They could really mix up their identities and we'd never know who is who, especially under a mask and costume."

Rein lifted an eyebrow, "Sounds like a splendid idea if you ask me."

Nicholas smiled, "I'm game."

Across the room, the others nodded and whispered among themselves.

Kristen and Kate seemed a little apprehensive of the thought, but finally shrugged and agreed.

Snow added, "Well, if we are helping them with their costumes anyway, then we should know who they will be."

"There ya go, Snow. Good point," retorted Jill.

Rein thought to himself how funny it would be if someone were to fool the girls by having someone else fitted for their costume, or even better ... have two men wear 'twin' costumes. Hmmm. Not a bad idea, as he smiled while pondering his clever plan.

Chapter 5
"Faeries and Princes"

It had been nearly a month since her arrival into the village and Snow was adjusting well to her new life. She enjoyed the company of her new women friends in the village. She considered them like sisters to her, the sisters she never had. And of course Stevie was like a brother to Snow. She felt very comfortable around him. He was very non-threatening, so to speak. She was feeling more comfortable with the things they did in the village. And she was still smiling at the most wonderful gift the men bestowed upon her yesterday. A treehouse of her very own! How thoughtful! Stevie's idea, no doubt. It was built in the very oak tree she escaped in that first day. It was lovely and very efficiently crafted. It was simple, yet elegant. It consisted of one room, a split level. The ground ladder led up to a small porch with a front door. You walk directly into the 'kitchen', a collection of cabinets and drawers mainly. There was a small metal inset for a fire one could use in keeping warm or to cook something small. Another small ladder led up to the half-level loft, the bedroom. This was just enough room for a feather bed, and of course a curtain to pull for privacy. Under the loft, an entire section of nothing but pillows, for a floor-type couch. Of course, she would still use the girls' cabins to take a bath or the like. She loved it, nonetheless. It was another way for her to stay close to nature, and a time to herself when needed.

She had been able to keep her journeys to the river a secret up until now. She preferred that the girls not know about her visits with Edward, since they seemed so against her seeing him for whatever reason. Last night Donnie managed to burst her bubble by ordering that no women go into the woods alone, not even during the day. Who did he think he was? Snow wondered if maybe this was a personal attack on her in order to totally take all of her freedom and privacy away, knowing how important nature was to her. But he couldn't know that. He didn't know her at all, and Snow wanted to keep it that way. He reminded her too much of those palace guards that used to make her shudder.

Snow shook off such thoughts, as she snuggled with her favorite rabbit, Whitey. He sat just as still as you please in Snow's hands, as if he knew she wouldn't harm him. What to do now? She wanted to keep visiting Edward at the river, or anywhere, when she could. Although, she didn't really know why. She was fond of Edward, but her feelings for him weren't ... well, she didn't seem to feel about him like she did for ... oh Snow, stop! There you go again. It's your imagination. Edward is a fine fellow. Of course, you know the real reason you visit him. But things will get better. They have to. You just have to get to know him better, that's all.

"Furry little thing isn't he?" Snow was startled by the soothing voice of Mitch.

She turned to him and smiled, halfway embarrassed that she had just been thinking about him. "Hello, Mitch." She swallowed, trying to recover, "Yes, he is my favorite. I call him Whitey. Not very original, I know."

Mitch laughed, "No, it's very cute, really. I thought I might find you here. I was about to start preparing dinner. Everyone's in the main hall discussing the festival and costumes and such. Thought you might like to join in."

Snow smiled as she put Whitey back in the rabbit pen, " Oh, yes, I would. How thoughtful of you. I hope you aren't slaving away over that hot stove so much so that you can't join in the discussion."

Mitch winked at her, "Nah, I'm sure I'll get to put in my two bits worth." Mitch offered her his arm and she took it as he led her back to the dining room.

In the room, she found everyone discussing their costume choices and other plans for Halloween night.

"Hey, Thomas, why don't you go as the "Headless Horseman"? teased Ivan as Thomas replied with a hard 'look' and added,

"Well, how about you being ol' Robin Hood?"

Ivan retorted, "Actually, I had been thinking more along the lines of the 'Black Knight', but Robin Hood wouldn't be so bad. He was an excellent marksman."

"You knew Robin Hood?" gleamed Snow, " I just adore archery."

Kate eyed her quizzingly, "Snow, you can shoot a bow and arrow? I would never have guessed. I'd love to see you shoot sometime."

"Sorry, I'm late, everyone." Murray burst in. "Had to bring Mitch the dinner to cook tonight. It was my turn to do the hunting. Not much luck, though. Had to use a couple of our own critters. Don't worry, Kate. It wasn't your pig, Brutus," added Murray, with a look at Kate.

"Yeah, Kate. Are you going to be dressing up that beast Brutus for Halloween, by the way?" laughed Ivan. Kate just looked at him.

"That reminds me," Snow added, "I'm going to be gathering materials and such and need to know what all you would choose in the way of costumes."

Stevie said shyly, "Well Snow, I don't wanna be no trouble, so I thought I'd just cut some 'oles in a sheet and be like a ghost, ya know? That'd be easiest."

Snow smiled at his courtesy, "Oh Stevie, you know you're no trouble, but if that's what you'd like to do. I'm sure we can arrange that."

"Eddy and I will get with you later about our costumes," Rein smiled mischievously as he went over the plans in his head to have a little fun this particular 'Hallow's Eve'. He had asked Eddy what he thought about having 'matching' costumes of a sort. Eddy had agreed thinking it might be a fun idea. Rein formed the idea after a most enlightening conversation with Duncan the other day about a certain 'royal decree'. When Duncan pondered the idea of Snow's visits in the woods with Eddy, he mentioned that Yolanda struggled with telling Snow the truth about Eddy and could never quite get the words out.

Curious about the situation, Rein decided to take a stroll in the woods and sure enough, found Snow and Eddy fishing by the river's edge. He couldn't help but laugh to himself at how dry the conversation was, and how bored Snow actually appeared, resting her face in her hands, fishing pole on her knee as she listened to Eddy go on and on about fishing and hunting and the like. Of course funnier still was that Eddy wasn't even as good of a fisherman as Rein was, who had decided to give it a rest when Eddy took a fancy to it. All this talk about 'royal decree' and this and that was just plain hogwash, thought Rein. That was the reason for the matching costume idea. His thought was maybe he could get Snow to see that a 'true love' is not found within any decree, no matter how 'sacred' the tradition is. Besides, it should prove to be jolly good fun, anyway.

After dinner, Snow delighted everyone with a beautiful song. Mitch thought her voice was like an angel.

Everyone clapped when she finished.

Kristen offered, "Snow that was so beautiful! You know, I don't think anyone would mind if you sang for us every night!"

Mitch touched her hand, "You can definitely sing for me anytime you like."

Snow smiled, blushing.

"Dinner was delicious, as usual, Mitch. Thanks, man" sighed Nicholas as he reached for his cup.

"Murray, you said you didn't have much luck hunting. What did you finally come up with for dinner?" asked Trent.

"Well, luckily, we still have our little rabbit farm out there, so I gotta confess. Those two fat ones did us pretty well, the black one and that furry white one."

Snow gasped as if she'd been stabbed with a knife. "No!" she cupped her hands over her mouth to stifle a cry, jumped up from the table and ran outside.

"I wish you hadn't said that, Murray!" Added Mitch sadly as he too got up from the table and followed Snow outside.

"What did I say?" asked a confused Murray as he looked around the room.

Mitch found Snow huddled in a heap next to the dining cabin with her knees in her chest sobbing. Mitch crouched down next to her and gently stroked her arm.

She peeked out at him for a second and then buried her face again, embarrassed, "Why do I get so attached to animals? I know that their main purpose is for food for the village"

Mitch brushed back her hair, "Hey, I want to show you something, OK?" He spoke so gently that Snow looked up at him. He wiped one of her tears away, "Come on. It's alright." He took her arm and helped her to her feet. He led her to the back door of the kitchen and lifted a box onto one of the preparation tables. Then he raised the lid.

"Whitey!" Snow gasped with glee. She picked him up and held him in her arms close to her face, "Hello there," she said tenderly.

Mitch for a second wishing he were the rabbit, "I went and picked another rabbit when Murray brought him over. I would never cook him knowing how much he meant to you."

Snow looked at Mitch with regret remembering her thoughts of him just a few moments ago. She put Whitey back into the box and looked back at Mitch lovingly, "I'm sorry for doubting. I shouldn't have."

As she hugged him, he wished the moment would last for hours, "It's alright Snow. You didn't know. "

She pulled back and looked at him again, "I do now, " and she kissed him tenderly on the cheek.

"Aye, you alright, Snow? You ran outta there so upset. We all didn't know wha' ta think, ya know, " came Stevie's concerned tone suddenly.

"Thank you Stevie. I'm alright now. It's Whitey, see. I

thought they cooked him." She lifted the lid to reveal her furry friend to Stevie.

"Oh, yeah, I remember ya said ya liked him pretty good. I'm glad he didn't end up dinner, there."

Mitch thought for a second, then with a gleem in his eye, "Stevie, would you please be a dear and get Whitey back to the rabbit pen? I'm sure he's pretty tired after a scare like that."

Stevie nodded and took the box, "Sure thing. You're right about that. He's probably plum wore out from all that ruckus."

As Stevie took the rabbit back to its home, Snow smiled at Mitch, "Now you weren't trying to get rid of him, were you?"

Mitch looked shocked, "Of course not. I just know Stevie likes to help out in any way he can around here."
Snow eyed him suspiciously.

"Speaking of help, I'd better go and remind Trent that it's his turn to do the dishes tonight. Are you free this evening, Miss Snow?"

Thinking for a moment, "Well, other than speaking with Rein and Edward about their costumes, yes, I believe so."

'Rein again', thought Mitch ... 'great'! He would definitely rather be around if Rein was going to be paying her a visit. The fancy Rein had taken to her lately just seemed to be more than 'friendly' to Mitch's observation. He started, "Yes, costumes. I suppose I should think of something for the festival, shouldn't I?"

"Of course!" Snow cooed, "Why don't you come to the tree house and we will get you fixed up. We'll pick out something perfect I'm sure."

Happily, Mitch offered, "Great. I have been wondering how you fixed up the place."

Snow's eyes lit up, "Oh, it's simply wonderful. You all were such dears to build it for me."

"Well," Mitch's eyes looked down at the ground regretfully, "Actually I'm not too good with woodwork, so I can't take any credit. I'm more of a 'kitchen help' person I guess."

Snow smiled, "Well it does have a kitchen that could probably use a little help ... in stocking supplies, perhaps?"

Mitch caught her gaze lovingly, "I think I can do that." Snow found it difficult to tear her eyes away from his, but managed to do so. Mitch passed the reminder of the dishes to Trent and packed a basket of supplies for the tree house. Snow went ahead to separate out the materials she gathered before everyone arrived.

"Cheerio!" came Rein's voice at the bottom of the ladder accompanied by Eddy.

Snow's door was open and she peeked down the ladder, "Come on up. I've been expecting you."

Upon their entrance, they found Snow with piles of materials on her 'floor couch' pillows. "What did you fellows have in mind?"

"Well," Rein smiled, "we thought it would be fun to have matching costumes. Like what about the 'brothers Grimm'?" laughed Rein and Eddy while Snow stared at them blankly.

"The brothers what?"

"Never mind, " Rein continued, "We thought we would both be the 'grim reaper' in a black cloak and stocking caps."

Snow frowned, "You know, in a costume like that, it will be difficult to tell you two apart."

Rein grinned, "Exactly the idea. After all, it is a masquerade, right? Old Eddy and I thought we would have a bit of fun with everyone."

Snow was thinking how awkward this would be with Rein and Edward in the same costume. She decided that perhaps it would be best to stay away from the both of them the evening of the masquerade for obvious reasons.

Rein continued, "So what do you think, dear? Do you think there's enough black material for the both of us?"

Snow smiled shyly, "Yes, I'm sure we can find enough. Jill also has lots of material at her cabin as well."

"Well, we would rather our costumes be made by such a lovely princess as yourself, " winked Rein.

Snow fidgeted at Rein's flirtatious tone, mainly because it was appealing to her, and she didn't want it to be. Perhaps she'd rather the tone had come from Edward, but couldn't picture that it would have contained the same meaning, somehow.

"Evening, gents." Mitch announced loudly carrying a basket of supplies with one hand, while attempting to climb the ladder with the other.

Rein tried to hide his disappointment. "Oh hello, Mitch."

Eddy looked at the basket with curiosity, "What do you have there? More materials?"

"No, this is some supplies for Snow's tree house. Can't have her cabinets bare." Mitch set the basket down on the small countertop against the wall.

"Thank you so much, Mitch. Any thought yet as to what you would like to be for the masquerade?" Snow began sifting the black material out of the piles on her couch pillows.

Mitch came to have a look, "Well, what do you suggest?"

Snow sifted through the rest quizzingly, "Well, anything except black, I hope."

Mitch laughed, "Anything is fine I'm sure."

Snow turned to Rein and Eddy, "Oh, stocking caps. Can you be dears and see if Jill has two black stocking caps, or something I could make those out of?"

Mitch looked at Rein, "You guys robbing a bank?"

Rein smiled weakly, "No. Eddy and I are going to be the 'grim reaper', the both of us."

Eddy winked and motioned to Snow, 'Yeah, you know the 'brothers Grimm'?"

Mitch laughed, while Snow still appeared confused and shook her head as though she were fairly used to never getting the jokes around here.

A reluctant Rein along with Eddy left the treehouse in search of two stocking caps from Jill, leaving Mitch at the tree house with Snow. "What is such a beautiful princess as yourself going to dress as?"

Snow blushed, "Well, I don't rightly know yet, but I was

going to let it be a surprise when I'm finished."

Mitch teased, "Hmmm, I would think such a lovely princess would prefer to be accompanied by a prince at the masquerade?"

Snow was frozen as she stopped sifting through remnants. How did he know about that? Did Yolanda say something? What did he mean by that?

Seeing her discomfort, "Or are you not planning to dress as a princess?"

Snow gave a sigh of relief, "Oh, you mean a costume! Well, I haven't yet decided, really."

Mitch smiled nervously as he tried to think of a costume, since his first brilliant idea of a prince didn't seem to go over like he'd hoped.

"Are you saying you were thinking of dressing as a prince for the masquerade?" Snow asked quickly, trying to sound objective.

Mitch found a particular spot to stare at on her new wooden floor, "Oh well I was just thinking if you needed an escort. But I didn't know what you were going to dress as."

Snow gave him an eye, "I see. So the guys here gave you an idea to dress up in matching costumes as well, eh?"

Nervously, Mitch continued his fascination with the spot on the tree house floor, "Oh, well, only if you think it may be something you would like to do. But if not, it's no big deal, really."

Snow had finally caught his meaning, although she had been reluctant to admit it to herself what Mitch was doing. He was flirting with her. Although, one part of her desperately wanted to give in and flirt back, another part of her saw the danger in it and said 'no'. Was it sincere, she thought? Of course, Mitch is always sincere. Why not? It's a party, right? She decided to meet herself halfway in between. "Well, I had thought about making wings from mesh and chicken wire as I've always dreamed of what it would be like to fly, so perhaps I will be a 'fairy princess'. However, I just don't think I can quite see you wearing wings, Mitch. Perhaps just a regular prince costume would suit you best."

Mitch raised his eyes to meet hers upon hearing her suggestion. He was thrilled. It sounded perfect to him. Their gaze met for what seemed to be hours, although Mitch knew it was only for a few seconds when he finally got the words out, "OK. A regular prince it is."

Both smiled and Snow again felt her feelings for Mitch deepening, something very difficult to fight when Mitch was looking back at her with his warm brown eyes and friendly smile. Mitch was finding that Snow's treehouse was quite a romantic setting. He wondered what her reaction would be if he kissed her at that moment. Her eyes seemed so friendly and her lips inviting, but he didn't want to approach the issue too soon, too soon for Snow that is. He had wanted to kiss her that moment she fell into his arms from the very tree they sat in now. How funny life was to bring them back here at this moment in this setting. Of course Mitch always considered himself a hopeless romantic. He loved cooking romantic dinners and serving fine wines and after dinner coffee. Mitch was finding the temptation more and more difficult to resist. Snow had kissed him on the cheek, earlier. He could just do the same. But could he stop with just a peck on the cheek with her lips only centimeters away? He thought, well, it would be worth a try. No, he should wait until the party at least. Shouldn't he? Maybe it wouldn't hurt, just a small ...

"Oi, Snow! Ya up there?" came the unmistakable voice of Stevie once again. "I got a sheet for my costume. Can ya believe this? Rein gave it to me at Jill's house just now. Wasn't that nice of him? He said I should bring it to you right away so you can have time to fix it up, like."

Mitch rolled his eyes, knowing Rein's sole mission was to send anyone or anything to spoil any time he might have with Snow. It certainly would not take her very long to cut a few holes in a sheet.

"Come on up, Stevie," laughed Snow, not noticing Mitch's disappointment.

"I'd better go and make sure Trent didn't make a complete

disaster area out of my kitchen." He paused to gaze into her eyes once again. "I'll see you tomorrow, fairy princess?"

Snow smiled and blushed as Mitch departed.

As it turned out, it only took Snow a few minutes to get Stevie's costume ready. What kept him there for the better part of the next two hours was a book that Stevie decided Snow really needed to hear.

"Are you kidding me?" came Jill's reaction as Yolanda told her of Snow's recent excursions.

Kate added "She's going for Eddy after all, is she?"

Yolanda frowned, "Now, you aren't supposed to know this. I wasn't supposed to say anything, but I just didn't know how to approach the situation. You know how sensitive she is. How do we tell her about Eddy? I don't think her time had a lot of that sort of thing. Homo--...well, you know?"

Jill thought for a moment, "Well, maybe we shouldn't tell her, then. Maybe we should try an experiment of sorts. I've always wondered if it would work on ol' Eddy boy, anyway."

Kristen frowned, "What are you talking about, Jill? You've got that mischievous sound in your voice that always scares me."

Kate added, "Yeah, what are you up to, Jill?"

Jill went to her room and came back with a very small vile of a liquid. "Here is a sampling of my 'Dixie Love Oil'. I say we let Snow give it a whirl on ol' Eddy dear. If it doesn't work, she's no worse off, but if it does ... well if Eddy is who she wants, then that's who she'll get, against my better judgment. But hey, it's her life."

Yolanda shook her head, "I dunno, Jill. It sounds too risky. Besides, I don't think Eddy is right for Snow. We just gotta get her to let go of that silly decree thing."

Jill brushed her hair off of her shoulders, "Well, we can't tell her what to do or who to see. She may be young, but she is still old enough to make her own decisions and her own mistakes as well."

Kate gave Jill a look, "Are you doing this to try to help Snow or just because you're curious of the oil's effects on someone like Eddy's persuasion?"

Jill smiled, "Well, of course I wanna help Snow. I already spoke my peace on how I think Eddy is all wrong for her."

Kristen added, "Well, we all think that. But the question is do we tell Snow what the oil does?"

Jill thought about this, "True. Well, then I suppose we should have a talk with her about it. I think she could handle it. And if she doesn't want to use it, that's up to her."

Kate nodded, "That sounds innocent enough."

Kristen agreed as well.

They all looked at Yolanda, still uncertain. She sighed and finally agreed, "Well alright, but just remember, this wasn't my idea."

Jill smiled, "No, I'll be takin' full credit for this one. My curiosity will probably get the best of me someday," as the girls all laughed.

The next morning, Snow felt as if her feet were simply floating through the orchard as she stared upward at the trees. The blossoms were now gone and the leaves were beginning to turn multiple colors of yellow and orange as one of them brushed against her hair. She had a dream last night, a wonderful dream. She was here in the orchard, just like she was now. Mitch was with her. But things were different, much different. In her dream, it was the Halloween festival and Mitch was dressed so handsomely as a prince, the prince of her dreams. Only in this dream, he WAS the prince of the Willows. She would no longer need to worry about her decree, that silly decree. Snow quickly apologized under her breath to her father for calling the decree 'silly'. But in her dream, she was so happy. She returned here to the orchard to, if just for a moment, pretend it were true. Her daydream was interrupted by the rumbling of her stomach. She hadn't had breakfast yet and she was starving. Apples! Over by one of the trees was a basket of apples that her prince ... er umm

... Mitch had no doubt been picking that morning. She loved apples and right on top of the bunch was an exceptionally large red one.

Just as she was about to bite into it, it was snatched out of her hands. "Whoa, wait Snow." Mitch's face looked almost white as he held the apple she was about to eat.

Snow felt a combination of confusion at Mitch's actions and dreaminess in seeing his warm smile so briefly after her previous night's dream about him.

Thinking quickly, "These haven't been washed, yet. But I have some nice clean peaches in the kitchen, probably the last ones till next year. They are just about out of season. You should get them while you can."

Snow smiled, "Sounds lovely."

Mitch felt embarrassed in taking the fruit right out of her hand, but he couldn't help but feel an uneasiness in watching Snow eat ... an apple. He knew it was silly, just a dumb story in a book, but he just didn't feel comfortable.

"OK Kate. Whatcha got up yer sleeve?" asked Stevie as he followed Kate into the orchard.

"There she is. 'Royal archery champion'!" said Kate when she saw Snow. "I found this set and wondered if you would do us the honors?" as she presented Snow with a bow and a packet of several arrows.

"Champion? Oh, Kate, I don't know if I'm that good. I'll probably disappoint you."

Mitch folded his arms, "Well, no matter what, I know you'll be better than me. I've never even picked up a set myself. Please go ahead. I would really like to see you shoot."

"Yes, please Snow," came a plea from Stevie with his begging eyes.

"Here, how about shooting at this." Mitch took an arrow and thrust it through one of the apples, then shoved into the tree bark.

"Well, alright, since you are all so insisting." Snow stepped back about six meters. She loaded the bow instinctively and shot at the apple. Bam! The arrow landed almost dead center.

"Oi, Snow! 'at's a dead target center there!" came Stevie's approval.

"Wow! I know who to get for my bodyguard, now." Mitch applauded.

"Well, maybe I was a little close, there. I'll step back a little more. I can't remember how far back I usually practice. I just shoot, is all."

She stepped back to about ten meters, loaded the bow and let the arrow fly. Splat! The arrow hit the apple once again, this time just off to the side, but still making its mark.

"Bravo, girl!" Kate clapped "You are really good at this. We should get a contest going at the festival and put you in it."

"Aye, Kate! That's a great idea! What if we was to 'ave a contest with teams and 'ave different games and stuff and prizes, like that. Ya think we could do that for the festival?" Stevie's begging eyes were directed at Kate this time.

Kate thought that this was perhaps one of Stevie's better ideas. "You know Stevie, that's a wonderful idea. I think that would be great fun, and I'm going to tell the others that it was all your idea."

Stevie beamed with pride and smiled at Snow, "Well I know this much, Snow. I wanna be on your team, eh?"

"Make that two," coming from Mitch's direction.

"Let's see what different games everyone can come up with and we'll put it all together. That reminds me," and with a gleam in Kate's eye, "Snow, did you decide on your costume yet? I thought maybe you'd like to join us girls in Jill's cabin and we can compare ideas?"

Snow giggled, "Well, yes, actually," she glanced at Mitch and then back at Kate, "I did think of something. But I hope you don't think it's silly."

Kate smiled, "Nonsense! Come on then. Let's go have a little ... girl talk. Shall we?"

Upon arriving at Jill's cabin, Snow and Kate found Jill, Kristen, and Yolanda picking through different remnants, swapping outrageous ideas and laughing.

"Can you picture Donnie in something like this?" giggled Jill.

Kristen and Yolanda laughed hysterically. Jill quickly shoved the remnant under the pile as Snow and Kate walked in.

"Picture Donnie in something like what?" demanded Kate.

"Oh nothing." Jill said innocently while Kristen and Yolanda struggled to stifle their laughter, and Kristen unintentionally let out a 'snort'.

Trying to change the subject, Jill approached Snow, "Ah, Snow. We're so glad you're here! Sit down, dear. Have you thought about what you'll wear at the festival yet?"

Snow was baffled at the way the girls were fussing over her. Snow never imagined that they had a plan of their own. "Well, yes. I've always wondered what it would be like to fly. I thought I could make a pair of wings out of material covered chicken wire and be perhaps a fairy ... or actually, 'fairy princess' as Mitch suggested. Is that really silly?"

Yolanda giggled, "No, that isn't silly at all, Snow."

Kristen's eyes widened as she stopped sifting through remnants, "As Mitch suggested, huh? What else did he suggest?"

Snow looked down shyly as she smiled, "Well, he wanted to go as matching 'prince and princess', but I didn't think he would look right wearing the fairy wings."

The girls all laughed, but Snow was clueless as to the meaning behind it.

Kristen grumbled, "A 'fairy' prince? Nope ... wrong person."

Kate gave her a 'shush' look.

"So what did you suggest back?" winked Jill.

"Well, I simply thought he could just go as a regular prince instead. What do you all think?" inquired a curious Snow.

"Oh, well I definitely think that would be a lovely costume," Jill started, "and also perfect for you. Let's see, how about this?" Jill pulled out a short white negligee.

Snow frowned, "That's really short, Jill."

"Of course," Jill continued, "You're a 'fairy' princess, not a regular one. Faeries wear shorter dresses, like Tinkerbell."

"Like who?"

"Tinkerbell was a magical fairy who wore really short dresses, that's all. Don't worry, you'll have something on underneath it, of course."

"Hey, Jill, maybe we could find something a little longer for her," inquired Kate, "We don't want to give her 'culture shock'."

"Or the guys, either," added Kristen, "Some of them still have problems with jeans, remember?"

"Nah!" came Jill's retort. "The festival will be a perfect place for everybody to just get a grip, then. Everyone will be in costume. It will be a time for everybody to just have fun and hang out ... well not literally of course," as Jill noticed Snow wincing at the length of the dress. Jill gave her some additional materials to build her wings with and extra trimming for the dress.

"Now, there is another issue we would like to talk to you about, dear ...." as she hid the potion vile behind her back.

Chapter 6
"Witches' Brew"

As Snow rubbed the vile in her fingertips, she pondered what the ladies told her. She had never heard of such a substance. "What do you think about it all, Tweety?" The little bird eyed her fingers as if he were inspecting them for food. "Sounds almost barbaric, but still interesting." She didn't have any immediate intentions on using the oil in the near future. She hadn't seen a need for such a thing. "It has always been within my heart to find a gentleman that will love me for who I am." Although the thought was an interesting concept, she thought it would be almost cruel for her to use a potion such as this on a gentleman. But still, she couldn't help but wonder what kind of effect it would have. Brushing away the thought, she tucked the oil away in a drawer, gave Tweety a little rub on the head, and then tucked herself away in her new loft bed.

"What about a 'witches' brew', Mitch?" inquired Jill as she helped him decide on the items to be served at the upcoming festival.

"A what?" as Mitch continued writing finger food ideas down on paper.

"A witches' brew! Ya know, a party punch that really packs a 'punch' ... has a kick to it?"

He nodded, "Oh, you mean 'spiked punch'?"

"Exactly! That's just what this festival needs! I mean Donnie already has us coming back in here at the end of the evening like prisoners. Might as well make the best of the situation with some interesting conversation, or possibly games and such over a good witches' brew." Jill reached down to pet her black cat that was affectionately rubbing against her leg.

Mitch shrugged, "I guess we can do that."

"So what ideas have we got so far in the way of Hallow's Eve treats for the festival?" as Jill leaned over to glance at his paper. "Oh, ya gotta add Dead Sea Soup. I can make that one."

Mitch eyed her with curiosity, "Dead Sea Soup, huh? OK, this I gotta taste for sure."

It was wolves. Wolves had been spotted around the village. They were getting braver as it was getting colder ... mostly at night. Therefore, Donnie demanded all residents stay indoors after dark. Hence, this is why everyone would need to stay in the main cabin that night ... festival or no festival. Plus, Donnie was skeptical that Halloween wasn't going to be such an uneventful night.

"That's it Tweety, that's the last step." As Snow came off of the final rung of the ladder to her treehouse. "Now it's off we go to find you some breakfast. How about some nice juicy worms, eh? Only for you would I go dig up worms, well and maybe for prince fishing ... I mean fishing with the prince, perhaps."

Carrying Tweety in a basket-made-bed, the little bird was still not able to fly. Snow made her way over to the rabbit and chicken pens where Edward kept his fishing gear usually. But it wasn't there.

"Wait a minute. He said he would wait for me. Surely, he didn't forget." She went around to the barn to see if he had left his equipment there and ran into Stevie.

"'allo, Snow. Whatcha doin' this mornin'?" came his usual happy tone.

"Have you seen Edward this morning, Stevie?"

"Oi, I seen him headin' toward his usual fishin' spot just a while ago. I guess we'll 'ave fish for dinner, eh?"

He did forget then, thought Snow as her lips involuntarily

curled into their usual pout.

"Aye, there. Wha' ya look so sad there for Princess? Did ya need to speak with 'im?"

"No, I just thought he was going to take me fishing with him, is all, since I can't venture into the woods alone due to Donnie's rules." She emphasized Donnie's name sarcastically.

"Aye, there Snow. No need ta worry. I'll take ya out there if ya'd like."

Snow's face brightened as though she'd walked into a surprise birthday party, "Oh Stevie, would you? That would be so lovely! Thank you!" She kissed him on the cheek, and he grinned, speechless.

"Hey, now. What's this?" Mitch had come around the corner to get some more canning jars he'd stashed in the barn. He teased them knowing Stevie was harmless, "Stevie, all the men are going to be jealous of you there, if you're not careful."

Stevie didn't catch that Mitch was just kidding, "Oi, Snow just wanted to go fishing with Eddy, but he forgot to wait for her and I just offered to take her to where he usually goes, that's all. Ya know, since the girls can't go out into th' woods alone from wha' Donnie said and all."

Snow looked down at the ground refusing to meet Mitch's suspicious gaze. 'I wish he hadn't spilled all of that,' thought Snow. She didn't really want to advertise her visits with Edward, especially to Mitch, of all people.

Mitch, in seeing her uneasiness with Stevie's explanation, "So, Snow you enjoy fishing?"

Snow petted the little bird in her basket and managed a shy reply, "Well, yes. I do find it quite relaxing."

Mitch never got a response look back from Snow, "Well, I was just after some more canning jars. A harvester's work is never done. See you all at lunch, then."

Snow barely heard a word Stevie said as they trekked into the woods toward the river. She was too lost in her own thoughts, her own feelings of guilt, or was it more of regret?

Here just the night before, she had planned to be a fairy princess to Mitch's prince and then she is caught red-handed in her schemes to visit Edward. 'You idiot!' Snow thought, 'if you had just played it cool and not acted like it was such a big deal, Mitch never would have known. But no! You had to go and not even look at him, like the cat that ate the bird, or um, mouse. Sorry, Tweety.' She glanced at her feathered friend in the basket. And in fact she was regretting the whole thing, now. Fairy princess with her prince ... she only wished. Only wished like in her dream that Mitch was the prince, the real prince. OK, that's enough, Snow. You really must get over these little 'pitty parties' you keep having for yourself. What's done is done. You can't change what's here. A dream is a dream and what's real is what's real. Everything else is....

"Snow?" Stevie had stopped and was looking at her with a questioning stare. "Did you hear what I said, Snow? Are you alright?"

Snapping back to where she really was, "Oh, yes. Sorry, Stevie. I guess I'm still sleeping this morning."

"'Ats alright. It wadn't important anyway."

"Hark, who goes there? I hear voices." Eddy teased.

"It's me, Stevie, and I've got Snow with me. Did you forget to take her with you this morning?"

"Stevie!" said Snow embarrassed.

"Oh goodness, I'm so sorry, Snow. You're exactly right. I forgot all about the fact that you can't go into the woods alone, after the 'world according to Donnie' talk there the other night. Here I was, expecting you to pop along any minute. I suppose it's too early in the morning for me today. Please have a seat, both of you."

Snow was relieved as she felt those blasted butterflies leave her stomach as they so often come to visit her. So he DID expect me, Snow thought. And I was afraid he had forgotten.

"What have you got there? A little visitor?" Edward peered curiously into the basket.

"I brought Tweety with me today. Would you happen to

have a tiny little extra worm you could spare?"

Edward smiled, "Of course. The fish don't much go for these little ones. He can have as many as he likes."

"Stevie!" came the booming voice of Donnie. "I thought I saw you trek into the woods with the pr---with Snow, that is. I'm glad you're heeding the warning, miss."

Snow refused to look at the barbarian and continued to feed her bird.

"No never mind, I don't need any acknowledgement from ya. Just so ya know that I'm watching ya Princess. I know how ya like to go strolling by yourself. But just remember, it's for your own good. Don't leave here alone without Eddy, now. Got that?"

"Don't worry, I wouldn't dream of it!" Snow finally glared back at him.

Donnie grinned and shook his head, amused at the girl's defiant spirit against his own authoritative nature. Maybe she had some guts after all, he thought. "Stevie, I wondered if you might come and help me with a couple of things back at the village."

Stevie followed Donnie like a puppy, as usual.

Hmmm, Snow thought. Donnie actually did me a favor today, and without even knowing it.

After a few moments' pause, a rather uncomfortable one at that, Snow managed, "Edward, what was your life like before you came here to the Willows? Did you have a family?

"Oh, yes, I did have a wife and son, respectively the queen and prince along with me and my brother."

Snow looked out onto the water. "So they were your last memory of home, then?"

Edward winced at the thought, "No, not exactly. I'd rather prefer to not think about my last memory of home, actually. But yes, I guess they were part of the whole picture."

Snow made designs in the dirt with a stick, "Do you miss having a family, or a companion, for example?"

Edward thought for a second, "Well, not really. Since I arrived here in the village, I have found the other men to be like brothers to me. They have actually become my new family, new companions. So I guess the answer to that is no," he added innocently.

"So you don't miss having a wife or child, then?" Snow kept her gaze on her dirt art below.

"Not really, no. It's kind of nice to have the freedom to just be me for a change. I don't have to worry about the responsibilities of wearing a crown here in the village. I'm part of a team here where we are just trying to survive."

She looked up from her artwork, "If I may be so bold, as to get your thoughts on the recent arrivals to the village … namely, us girls?"

Edward tilted his head, keeping his eyes on the fishing lure out in front of him, "Oh, it's a fine thing, I suppose. We could use a woman's touch around here on some things. Plus, it doesn't hurt to have some help doing chores and cooking and such. But I'm sure I have a different take on the idea than the other men. No doubt, some of them are interested in one thing or another, like being in the company of a woman and the like. But I'm just not after those kinds of things at this point in my life right now, you know? I can only guess that you aren't the type of girl that likes being 'chased' by different men, so you can feel safe with me. I would never do that sort of thing. That is what you were getting at, wasn't it? In no certain terms, right? You needn't worry. You're safe from being 'hunted' around me, so to speak."

"I appreciate that … uh, I suppose." Snow felt the butterflies had returned, and brought their friends this time. Great, she thought. That's just what she wanted to hear, sure thing Ed. I wonder what that's all about? Perhaps he had a bad relationship with the queen that left a bad taste in his mouth, thought Snow. Maybe she should go have another talk with Yolanda and see if she will tell her more this time … more about what is really going on with Edward. Then again, maybe Edward just needed a little 'push' …. like from a certain potion, perhaps? Stop it, Snow. You're not going to use that stuff. I'll bet this wouldn't be so difficult with Mitch. Oh, there you go again with the pity party thing! Quit it!

Edward began to pack in his gear, "Well, I guess we won't be having fish tonight. Doesn't look like they're biting today. They will probably be serving lunch soon. Ready to go back?"

Snow smiled weakly, "Sure." She scooped up Tweety as they hiked back to the village. Snow felt the pout try and return to her lips, so she bit her bottom lip to keep Edward from seeing. Not wishing to speak at all on the way back, lest she give away her disappointment somehow, she asked Edward if he knew what were the different types of trees they passed on their way back to the village. That way, the rest of the hike was composed solely of Edward pointing and reciting the different types of trees and what kinds of spores they produced. Perhaps it had been a silly question, thought Snow, but she didn't care.

Snow found Mitch in the kitchen preparing chicken for lunch that day. "Do you need a hand, there Mitch?" Snow looked at him with pleading eyes.

"Sure, why not. I'd always accept an invitation from you, Snow."

She blushed, "Well, I'm afraid we just didn't catch anything at the river. I just thought I'd tag along this morning. You know, trying to get the hang of fishing and getting to know everyone and, well, you know, everything else like that." Golly, Snow you're rambling! He's really going to think you're batty, now!

"Snow, you surely don't have to explain yourself to me, love. Besides, you know I'd never worry about Eddy of all people," he laughed.

Now, what did he mean by that? Why not worry about Eddy? What was the deal with everybody regarding Edward!? Alright, now I have to find out, thought Snow.

After lunch, Snow couldn't find Yolanda, but Stevie suggested they go for a walk into the woods, as he wanted to look for 'scary looking' branches to decorate with for the festival.

"Oi, here's some over 'ere. These look pretty scary, don't they Snow?"

But Snow didn't hear Stevie. She was too preoccupied with a strange mist over in a small clearing ahead. She stepped closer and an eerie feeling came over her.

"Aye, Snow ya alright? Ya sleeping again are ya?" Stevie teased. But as he came closer to her, he could see her face was almost white, her complexion paler than usual, her wide-eyed expression directed in the distance toward the misty clearing.

"Stevie, what's over there?" pointing to the clearing a few meters away.

"Wha'? Well I'll be!! Ya know what tha' is? 'Ats where I found you Snow! Right there in 'at pile of leaves!" He walked towards the clearing.

"No, Stevie, I don't have a good feeling about what's over there."

"It's alright Snow. I've been 'ere 'undreds of times."

Snow reluctantly followed him over to the familiar pile of leaves she began her quest into this new life from.

"See 'ere, Snow. You 'ad to 'ave fallen from outta this tree, maybe. There's no other place you could've come from."

Behind the leaf pile, stood a large tree ... an odd-looking tree with a hollow area at the bottom. Snow wouldn't get too close to the area. She felt a breeze on her face mixed with the mist in the air and she began to hear something in the wind, a voice almost. It was saying something. It was speaking her name ... she would swear to it!

She grabbed Stevie's arm, "Come on, Stevie. Let's go."

Stevie was peering into the hollow bottom of the tree, "No, let's 'ave a look and see if we can see where you came from, eh?"

The voice in the wind was getting louder saying her name over and over.

She tugged at Stevie's arm, an urgency rising in her voice, "No, come on! We gotta go NOW!!"

"It's alright Snow. We're not gonna be late for supper, promise."

She let go of Stevie's arm and backed away from the tree, feeling the mist all around her. It was the same mist that followed her through the enchanted forest as she ran from the huntsman, from her stepmother. She tried to tell Stevie to hurry, but she couldn't speak, she couldn't breathe. What was wrong? She was choking! She tried to gasp, but couldn't. She grabbed her throat. On the outside it felt normal but on the inside, her airway felt blocked. She couldn't get any air at all! 'Stevie HELP!' she thought. She couldn't get his attention. She ran out of the clearing, out of the mist and fell to the ground gasping for air finally able to breath. She clawed at the leaves on the ground as she caught her breath. In her grasp she clutched a large broken branch. She held it for what might come after her, out of the clearing. Whatever that was, she was ready in case it materialized again. She got up, still not able to speak, and so she ran. She ran back to the village as fast as she could. Stevie or not, she had to get away from there, away from whatever that was, choking the life out of her.

"Snow, would you look at this? Where do ya suppose this came from?" He turned around, but Snow was not there. "Snow? Where are ya? Snow!!" Frightened that she was in the woods alone, he knew he had to go after her. He went to put the object he just discovered into his pocket, then stopped to look at it once more and wondered if it's purpose had anything to do with Snow in relation to the story behind the fairy tale. He rubbed the shiny object in his fingers, then put it in his pocket, carefully. He didn't want to cut himself ... on the broken piece of a mirror he had just found inside the tree.

Chapter 7
"All Hallow's Eve"

Snow was putting the finishing touches on her costume. Made from the short satin slip given to her by Jill, Snow had lined the outside with sheer white chiffon and added a large ruffle with a silver ribbon at the bottom of the satin garment. The small straps of the slip were now covered with a lovely lace. Snow also added more strips of lace across the rest of the shoulder down to the arm, giving the dress the look of five straps on the shoulders. Along the neckline, a trim of lace with a silver ribbon to match the hem. Her wings were crafted with chicken wire, covered with white chiffon, and also trimmed in lace and silver ribbon. Of course, pinned to the center of her neckline was her most prized possession, her family crest. As an added touch to her fairy princess costume, she had fashioned a crown of flowers that she had picked near the edge of the woods and fastened it with chicken wire. Hanging down from the back of the crown were the lace and silver ribbons she had used in her costume.

Snow held the costume up for Kate to see, "Are you sure you don't think it's too short? That garment Jill gave me ... what was it called again? A negli ... what?"

"Negligee," finished Yolanda.

"Yes, that was it. I just thought it was really short, so I added some more material to the bottom, here."

Kate stood up and spun around in her pretty witch costume, "Well Snow, look. Mine is even shorter than yours, so you don't have to worry. The men will all be staring at me instead," and she gave a wink to Kristen who smiled and shook her head.

"Well, that's good I suppose, because Donnie says it isn't good for me to 'flunte' around the gentleman with not a lot of clothing on."

"Flunte? Oh, you mean 'flaunt'! Flaunt around!" laughed Kate.

Kristen gave an irritated look at Snow's statement, "Snow, don't you listen to Donnie. He's just talking to hear himself talk most of the time," with a sideways glance at Kate.

"Ta da!" Jill burst through the door ceremoniously in a lovely crushed green velvet dress. It had a 'southern belle' style to it, like 'Scarlett O'Hara', Jill had hinted. Of course Snow had no idea who 'Scarlet O'Hara' was.

"Well, what do you think?"

"I think somebody will have to hold Roger down when you enter the party, dear!" said Yolanda teasingly.

"Wow, that's lovely, Jill. I really think I should have gone with a longer dress, like back home," as Snow looked at Jill's long green dress, "However, I made this hooded cape much like one I had at home. Perhaps I'll just leave it on all night."

Kristen gasped, "Snow, no! You can't do that! You worked so hard on your dress. It's lovely, and it isn't that short, really. And what about your wings? The cloak will cover your pretty wings. You have to take it off sometime."

"Well, I'll think about it. I guess," as Snow wrapped the white cloak around her shoulders.

"Aye, ya girls in there?" came Stevie's voice with a knocking at the door. "All the chores are done now, and Donnie says we can start the games and stuff for the party! Are ya ready yet?"

"Poor Stevie, I think he's just about ready to jump out of his skin. He's been waiting on this party all week. I'll bet he didn't sleep a wink last night." Kate whispered, then continued to Stevie, "Yes, Stevie. We're all about done. Tell all the guys to meet us in the main hut. We'd prefer to make a, " she paused to think, "...ceremonious entrance."

Kate looked to Yolanda who giggled and to Kristen who gave a 'thumbs up' signal. Snow looked at Kristen's thumb wondering if she was hurt.

All of the food was prepared and laid out. Mitch was relieved that he wouldn't have to spend the better part of the festival in the kitchen. He was also glad he hadn't spilled anything on the handsome royal blue velvet 'prince' costume that Snow had made for him. When he picked it up at her treehouse that morning, Stevie was there as usual. He knew that Stevie's relationship with Snow was harmless, but he couldn't help but be jealous. At least, he hoped their relationship was harmless, he thought. Perhaps he should watch their progression more closely. After all, there is a first for everything.

All the men waited in the main hall. It was just about noon-time. Ivan adorned a handsomely formed armor of chain mail with a black crest. Just as he had hinted the other evening, he was the 'Black Knight'. He said it was someone he once knew and greatly respected. Thomas did not come as the Headless Horseman, but as a hooded priest or monk ... minus the bald head. Stevie was of course in the 'ghost' sheet that Snow cut out for him, although Rein and Nicholas batted around the idea that he should have been Snow's court jester. Stevie had not quite understood their meaning, and Donnie melted away their teasing with a hard stare.

Nicholas chose the easy route and decided to be a hunter, in his usual attire and unloaded hunting rifle. Rein and Eddy wore the matching grim reaper or otherwise known as 'Brothers Grimm' idea that Rein conjured up for Snow to make them. Trent had decided to be a vampire. He said it was a great excuse to be able to bite the ladies on the neck. His statement received groans from the other men in the room. All of the men could hardly wait to see what the ladies were wearing. Their imaginations ran wild when Stevie came in with his announcement of the girls' entrance shortly.

The CD player 'boom box' was already playing party music awaiting any 'willing soul' to come and dance to its tune. The door to the main hall opened and the men were almost tempted to hold their breaths as the ladies strolled in. Upon seeing such visions of loveliness, it almost took their breath away after all. Even in their 'masquerade masks' it was evident who was who. Stevie all but bounded over to Snow to tell her how lovely she looked. Duncan immediately approached Yolanda and took her hand and kissed it. Her Renaissance noblewoman attire was perfect with his handsome British uniform. Roger quickly followed and asked Jill to dance. After thinking for a second just to torture him, she said 'yes'. As they joined Duncan and Yolanda, Murray took a quick look around the room to be sure no one was going to try and beat him to the punch to ask Kristen to dance, and then strolled over to ask her. Dressed to dance donning her 1920's flapper dress, she pondered maybe there were some early 20th century jazz CD's in the collection.

Stevie wasn't very comfortable at dancing, so instead he offered to get Snow some punch. Seizing his opportunity, Mitch quickly headed in Snow's direction, so as not to give an open door to Rein to dance with Snow first. But it was too late. Rein had appeared almost out of nowhere and asked Snow to dance.

Snow gave a look of concern, still thinking about the fact that she would rather not remove the cloak she wore to hide the revealing nature of her costume. "Well, I'm not sure I'm very familiar with the way everyone dances here. I'm sure it's quite different than I am used to."

Rein smiled at her innocence, "That's alright sweetheart. I'll teach you everything you need to know."

Although she was reluctant, Rein took her hand and started to lead her over to where the others were dancing.

As Snow took a step and turned around, Stevie was coming towards her with a cup of punch for her. They collided and punch flew all down her cloak. "Snow, oh dear I'm s' sorry! I go' punch all over yer pretty white cape!"

"Not to worry, it will wash out I'm sure. Here, Mitch can rinse this out for you. Can't you Mitch?" assured Rein as he untied Snow's cloak before she knew what was going on. As Rein removed the cloak, Snow's fairy princess costume was revealed.

Up until now, Snow had never worn anything that hadn't come to her ankles, at least. And now she was wearing a dress that hardly even came to her knees. Realizing she wasn't wearing the cloak now, she stuttered that she could still wear the cloak, punch and all. She turned and found herself face to face with Mitch. As he looked at her, he sighed. She was a vision. The soft skin of her face matched that of her legs and shoulders as he admired the way the lace draped her arms, and the way the ruffle of her homemade dress kissed her legs.

"Aye, Snow! I like yer costume better without that cape, anyway. And I love the wings ya made! 'Ats chicken wire in there, right?" As Stevie wiggled her wings, she turned and saw his fascination with her flying apparatus, and she felt a little more at ease, that perhaps not everyone in the room was staring at her naked legs after all.

"Here you go Mitch. Please be a dear and go wash out this cloak for Snow would you? I haven't a clue where you keep the soap flakes in that kitchen of yours, man." Rein shoved the cloak at a very annoyed Mitch and took Snow's hand. "Now, how about that dance?"

As Snow danced with Rein, she remembered back to their last dance in the barn and what happened afterwards. And it was difficult for her to look into Rein's eyes. She was afraid she would see something... something she saw that day that would allow her to let her guard down. And she didn't want that to happen again.

Mitch went to the back to put Snow's cloak in some soap and water. As Kate giggled at Mitch's obvious annoyance, she noticed Donnie's eyes on her. Truth was, he hadn't taken his eyes off of her since she came into the dining room.

She looked at him quizzingly, "Well, aren't you going to ask me to dance?"

"Later Angel," he winked. "Right now I think we'd all better get on with the games outside. There will be plenty of time later for dancing..." he paused to look Kate over for a second, "or whatever."

The afternoon was filled with delightful games of fun and competition. The 'pumpkin carving' award went to Stevie after much discussion. The winner of the 'bobbing for apples' went to Bart, especially since the ladies forfeited so as not to ruin their makeup. 'Knife throwing' went to Donnie hands down whereas the 'rifle target shoot' went to Nicholas. The 'archery contest' was very close with first place going to Snow, and Edward coming in a close second. There were many games that afternoon until it was suggested that they start the indoor games as it was starting to get dark.

As they headed inside, Snow happened to overhear a conversation between Kristen and Kate about a date Kate had with Mitch a few months back, before Snow came to the Willows. Once Kate admitted that it was Mitch's idea, Snow didn't want to hear anymore and went on inside, disheartened somewhat. Could Mitch still have feelings for Kate? After all, Snow was having her own troubles trying to get over feelings for some of these men, and she had just met them practically. So it seems totally possible. Snow, you've got to get a handle on things, it doesn't matter. 'Remember,' she thought to herself as she stroked the crest pinned to the center of her dress. Then she placed her hand in the pocket she added to the dress. She just wanted to be sure that it was still there. She stroked the little vile of 'Dixie Love Oil' as she remembered the words of the other women. Should she use it, Snow thought? Would it even work on Edward at all? And if it did, what kind of effect would it have? She wasn't sure if she wanted to use it here at the party, but she brought it just in case.

"Would you like some punch?" Rein startled Snow as she turned to see him holding out a cup to her. "Yes, thank you." She took the cup and smiled shyly. He looked at her lips as she smiled, and remembered how soft they were when he kissed her in the barn that day. He wished he could find a moment to try it again. Of course, perhaps he would be lucky enough to get to kiss her during the 'spin the bottle' game that evening, but mainly he wanted to find a moment alone with her sometime that night.

The 'spin the bottle' game was an unusual concept that Snow had not heard of. To spin a bottle and kiss a person whether you like them or not was a strange idea, but nevertheless, she reluctantly agreed to play. She thought, why not? 'After all, they all seem to look like the prince of my dreams, anyway.' As she was preparing to find a spot to sit, she noticed Edward's cup unguarded and took the vile out of her pocket. After a second's thought she hesitated but then remembered her father's decree. She tipped a little of Jill's potion into it, but not too much. She wanted to use just enough to see what it would do. She then decided to sit exactly across from Edward to make it easier for her to tell if it was working.

However, Snow noticed that throughout the game, Edward was more of a 'sipper' rather than a 'drinker', just taking little sips of his cup every so often. Snow thought to herself, 'it will take all night for this stuff to take effect.' After a few bottle spin rounds and a few cups of punch, Snow got up to get herself another cup, but fell back to the floor where she had been sitting.

"You alright Snow?" asked a concerned Stevie.

"Yes, I must have just tried to get up too quickly. That's all."

"No, it's probably the cups of punch you've been drinking there, dear," winked Kate. "It's spiked you know."

"Spiked? What does that mean?" Snow tried once again to rise to her feet, and she succeeded this time.

"It means the stuff's got spirit in it." Muttered Jill as she spun for her turn.

"She means rum, Snow," Edward clarified as he got up to give her a hand. "Would you like me to get you another cup?"

"No, maybe I shouldn't have any more then, " Snow smiled at Edward's courtesy.

"Nonsense! It's a party, girl! Woooohooooo!" Jill wailed as her bottle stopped at Roger. "Ya gotta live it up, Snow! Dance it up, drink it up!"

Kate spoke up, "Snow, don't worry, we'll make sure you don't go toooo overboard."

"Well, OK, " Snow turned to Eddy, "I guess it would be OK if I had just one more then."

Rein looked on Eddy's attentiveness to Snow with concern. Amazingly enough, during her turns, Snow's bottle never stopped on Rein or Mitch. It did however stop on Eddy, to Snow's delight. And to her surprise he gave her quite a large kiss. That stuff must be working, she thought!

On her next turn, the bottle stopped on Stevie. Beet red in the face, he looked down and laughed nervously, "What do I do?"

"Ya kiss her, ya nitwit!" yelled Donnie, followed by a roomful of laughter.

Without really looking at her, Stevie hesitated as he leaned into Snow, who smiled at his shyness and kissed him on the cheek. Just then Duncan came in from watch duty, "Who's next on watch?" Quickly, as if he'd been rescued from an awkward moment, Stevie jumped up, "It's me! I'm next on watch, Duncan!" And he quickly headed out the door.

The room was filled with laughter as stories of past memories and embarrassing moments became the topic of choice. Snow found herself giggling more than usual and finding an extra added comfort in being around everyone. Also, due to the punch she felt a strange giddiness that she wasn't quite used to and found herself gazing quite often between Eddy, Mitch and Rein, who she found were gazing back.

The dancing went on into the night and the music choices ranged from rock and roll to waltz to slow dancing. Mitch finally got his chance to ask Snow to dance. There was a lovely slow song playing that set a romantic mood for everyone in the room. As Mitch held her in his arms, he felt just how incredibly soft her satin costume was, or was it Snow that was so soft? Her hair smelled wonderful. Was it honeysuckle or vanilla? Perhaps it was both, Mitch didn't care. He just knew that the 'fairy princess' was dancing in his arms. The tune was familiar to Snow as she had heard it played by the ladies before, and she began to hum to the music. Mitch found her voice lovely and soothing, almost entrancing. The song was over just as soon as it had begun, or so it seemed for Mitch and Snow.

A medieval folk song began to play that was familiar to both Snow and Ivan. As they began to dance to the upbeat melody, they invited the others to join in and taught them the steps to the folk dance. All were in good spirits.

At one point in the evening, Nicholas reached for his glass on the fireplace mantle and accidentally knocked off the basket that Snow's pet bird Tweety was in. Just before the basket crashed to the floor, the little bird clumsily flew out of the basket and over to the end table by the door.

"Tweety! You flew! You can fly! Good Tweety!!" squealed Snow as she clapped her hands.

"Snow, why did you bring the bird to the party?" asked an annoyed Nicholas as the bird scared the daylights out of him when it almost crashed into his head.

Stevie, who was on watch outside peered in the door to see what all the fuss was about, "Aye! What's goin' on in 'ere? I 'eard some ruckus!"

Just then the bird flew out the door. "Tweety!" screamed Snow as she ran after him through the door and past Stevie.

Rein followed her, "It's OK, Stevie. I'll go and get her. You just keep on your watch."

"OK Rein. Just be sure that she don't go far!"

Rein pulled his black cap over his head to cover his short hairstyle and only revealing his face. When he and Eddy both did this, it was hard to tell them apart. Rein planned it this way. Perhaps now was the perfect time to take advantage of it.

"Ouch!" cried Snow as she tripped over the rocks by the side of the cabin.

"Are you alright?" Rein crouched near her when he heard her fall.

"Yes, I just scraped my knee. That darn punch won't allow me to keep my balance very well, you know?" Her words were slurred from the rum punch.

"Well, it isn't bleeding, so I guess we don't have to get the first aid kit," Rein assured as he rubbed her knee tenderly.

"But I have to find Tweety. I can't leave him out here all alone. He's just a baby." Snow's voice was filled with concern.

"It'll be alright. We'll find him, or I'm not Prince Edward."

Snow was somewhat startled, as she thought he was Rein, "Edward? How can I be sure you are Edward?" she halfway teased.

"Well, the other day at the river, remember how you told me about your sixteenth birthday? About how the kingdom of the House of Loring threw a joust tournament in honor of your birthday?"

Snow smiled and then paused for a moment, thinking. "Why did you follow me out here, Edward?"

"I wanted to be sure you didn't go off into the woods. You know it isn't safe."

Snow sighed not quite knowing what to say next, "Oh." As Rein brushed her hair from her face and continued to rub her knee, she thought how well the potion was working and she will have to try it again sometime when they aren't faced with a cabin full of people. Perhaps the next time they go fishing. Yes, that would be a good time to try it. They would be all alone. Rein touched her lips with his fingers and then moved in to kiss her, once again. Snow stayed still and after a second of their lips meeting, she kissed him back. Considering the tingling effect the rum had on her that night and especially at that moment, she began to wonder if someone had used the Dixie Love Oil on her. She began to feel a warmth in her stomach, but it wasn't butterflies this time. It was … different.

Rein moved from rubbing her knee to rubbing her upper leg. Snow flinched and backed away from the kiss. Then she thought that perhaps she shouldn't use the stuff when it was just the two of them after all. Perhaps it was too strong.

Rein removed his hand from her leg, "I'm sorry, I guess I got a little carried away. Please forgive me."

This gentlemanly statement of his made such an impression on

Snow that she leaned in to kiss him all on her own. Or perhaps it was the rum that had made the impression, but nevertheless Snow thought that she had finally gotten her prince. That Edward had finally fallen for her.

"Rein? Snow? Are ya over 'ere? Oh, good. I'm glad you found 'er, Rein. I was worried." Stevie had found the two over by the side of the cabin.

Snow frowned, "Stevie, this is Edward, not Rein."

"Well 'at's strange. I just spoke to Rein a moment ago when he went looking for..."

"We're fine, Stevie. Thank you," Rein interrupted trying to salvage his disguise. "You'd better get back to your watch, Stevie."

After Stevie had left, Snow stood up, "I trust Stevie, and you ARE Rein, aren't you? You tricked me!"

"Snow I can explain. I was only kidding. I was about to tell you, really."

Snow was furious, "Why would you say you were Edward? How would you know about my sixteenth birthday? You were spying on us the other day, weren't you? What else did you hear?"

Rein tried to hold her hands in his, but she pulled away. "Snow, I know that true love can't be found in any royal marriage decree no matter how sacred it is."

Snow's jaw dropped, "You must be eavesdropping on everyone in the village! Aren't you?"

"Snow, I wanted to show you what love really is. You aren't in your century anymore. You don't have to follow those silly rules."

"Silly rules! How dare you! That is my heritage and my family that you are calling silly! This conversation is over!"

Rein tried to say something else, but Snow ran away around to the back kitchen entrance and burst through the door. She shut it behind her and slid down to the floor sobbing.

Mitch had just come in to get some more cookies to fill the trays and was startled by Snow's entrance into the kitchen. He approached her and crouched down beside her, "Snow, sweet Princess, what's wrong honey?"

Through her sobs it was hard to understand her broken sentences, "Rein was Edward, but he wasn't, but I thought he was. He tricked me, he kissed me ... again. He knows about everything. Why? Why is this happening? Why am I here?" She began to sob uncontrollably.

Mitch pulled her into his chest to cry, "It's OK. It's going to be alright. You can cry. I don't mind. You can tell me everything. I'm a good listener. I hate to see you unhappy, Snow. You know that." He brushed her hair with his hands as she buried her face in his shoulder.

She stopped crying as Mitch held her closer to him. She felt that warm feeling in her stomach again. She remembered her dream again about how Mitch was the royal prince and how she had wished it were really so, just as she wished it now. She remembered that tonight he was supposed to be her prince, and she was his fairy princess. She pulled away enough to look into his eyes. She found that loving, soothing look he always had waiting for her when she would look into his eyes, even back when she fell into his arms out of the orchard or out of the oak tree, the one she now calls home. Home? Is this really her home now? She couldn't go back to her time, or she would surely be killed. Is this a place where she could be happy for the rest of her life? If she were with someone like Mitch, she could. With his soothing words, friendly smile and warm eyes, she felt safe, she felt loved. So there in the kitchen, she spilled everything to him. She told him of her decree and her recent outings with Edward in the hopes that he would see fit to form a union with her to satisfy her family decree. She told him what happened in the barn that night with Rein and also what had just happened before she came in here. She didn't, however, tell him of the Dixie Love Oil. Even with the liquor still clouding her head, she managed to still keep that a secret.

Of course Mitch was angry with Rein, but didn't show this to Snow. He was happy that she trusted him enough to tell him everything. He could also tell that the rum was still having its effects, and feared that this may have led to her kiss with Rein a few moments ago. Snow was vulnerable, too vulnerable. And Mitch didn't like the thought of anyone taking advantage of Snow in any way, no matter how small. He leaned down to wipe a tear off of her cheek and she looked up at him ... their faces, their lips almost touching. Once again he resisted the temptation to kiss her and merely smiled. She smiled back and kissed him on the cheek. In Mitch's thoughts he cursed that silly 'spin the bottle' game for the bottle not landing on him on any of Snow's spins.

She was looking deep into his eyes, "Why is it that you never kiss me, Mitch?" Snow slurred her words still struggling with the effects of the punch. "Do you not like me?"

Mitch was caught off guard and almost stammered his words at hearing her question, "No, dear. You couldn't be farther from the truth, sweet Princess. I ... I have wanted to kiss you since you first fell into my arms that first day, but I never allowed myself to do so. I know that you are from a different time and culture and that it is probably not considered a very proper thing where you come from. Is it?"

"Well," Snow looked at his costume, "since you are dressed as a prince tonight and I'm dressed as a fairy princess, we could just pretend for one night that it's proper, right? That you are my prince and I am your princess?"

Mitch wanted her words to be true so badly. He smiled, "Yes, that sounds lovely. Tonight is ours, Princess." He leaned in and kissed her gently. The warm feeling in her stomach spread quickly all the way down to her feet. As he kissed her, Snow touched his cheek, then brushed her hand through his hair. He pulled her closer, and put his arms around her, having to go underneath her wings.

The kitchen door opened, "Hey Mitch, did you ever find any more of those..." Kate's sentence trailed off as she saw Mitch and Snow on the floor by the back door.

Snow pulled away, upon hearing Kate's voice. Mitch jumped

up, helped Snow to her feet and began to stammer an explanation, "Snow is having a bit of a rough night. I was just trying to help calm her down, sort of."

Kate giggled, "Really, you don't have to explain anything to me. I'm just here to satisfy a sweet tooth. Please continue. I didn't mean to bother you."

Snow suddenly remembered what she overheard about them that afternoon. The rum was still kicking her emotions into overdrive ... the good ones and the bad, "No really it's alright. I'm sure Mitch here would much rather set up another date than listen to my sob stories all night. Excuse me." Snow walked back into the dining room, leaving both Mitch and Kate in the kitchen confused.

Snow went to a chair in a back corner of the dining room.

Edward spotted her coming out of the kitchen and went to her, "Snow, I've been looking for you. Are you alright?"

Snow turned away from him, "Leave me alone! You've done enough."

Edward looked puzzled, "What have I done?"

Snow snapped at him, "You tricked me! You pretended to be Edward, or have you forgotten already."

Eddy removed his black hood revealing the 'pageboy' hairstyle, "Pretended?"

Snow's eyes widened, "Edward, it is you! Oh I'm so sorry! Earlier, Rein tricked me into thinking he was you in order to..." Snow trailed off, having already said too much.

"In order to what, Snow?"

"In order to kiss me. That's what. There, I said it." Snow looked away.

Edward turned her face toward him, "So what you're saying is that you won't kiss him, but you will kiss me?"

Snow looked into his eyes, and couldn't speak without stuttering, "Well, um, yes, I ... I guess so."
"Why is that, Snow?"

She swallowed hard, "Well, because ... well, I don't know."

Eddy began to find her innocence quite appealing, and her appearance was lovely. Why hadn't he noticed before? He wasn't sure, but he noticed her now.

"Aye, Snow look! 'ere he is! Safe 'n sound, he is!" Stevie crouched down next to Snow's chair holding the smal bird.

"Tweety!" squealed Snow. "You found him! Oh thank you Stevie!" She kissed him again on the cheek, and this time he wasn't so embarrassed.

He really enjoyed Snow kissing him, actually. Then he remembered that he had brought that mirror piece to show Snow. He hadn't had a chance to tell her about it yet, and thought that the party would be a good place to show everyone. He thought that they all may find it interesting. But as he reached into his pocket to show her, it wasn't there. Oh no! It must have fallen out of his pocket sometime during the party. He began searching around the floor of the dining hall.

"Snow, could we talk outside?" asked Edward while Stevie was searching around Snow's chair.

"Well ya know I'd let ya on my watch, but it's Donnie's watch now, an' I' bet he won't let ya. I s'pose ya can try."

But Stevie was right. Donnie wouldn't let them go outside to talk, so Edward chose to speak with Snow in the kitchen. "I just wanted to find out more regarding what you told me in the dining room, but I thought it best we speak in private. I know that you probably didn't want everyone to hear. Is there something you want to ... tell me, perhaps?"

Snow looked down at the floor.

"Here you are," came Rein's voice coming through the kitchen door.

"Goodness, the kitchen is a popular place tonight." Snow sighed as she took a step away from them, her arms folded.

"Snow told me about what happened, Rein ... about how you tricked her. That wasn't a nice thing to do. Why would you do that?"

"You know, Eddy, I don't have to answer to you about anything I do."

Snow walked between them, "If you'll excuse me, I'm going to leave you gentlemen to talk, while Tweety and I take a little ... what's it called ... bathroom break, I believe?"

As Snow left, Rein continued, "Why do you care at all what Snow and I do, anyway?"

"Because whatever it was that you were doing, you were masquerading as me, which is the only reason she kissed you."

Rein glared back, "And what makes you think that?"

"Because she told me so, Rein!"

"And you expect me to believe that?" Rein turned and took a few steps away.

Edward walked toward him, "Yes I do. Stevie heard it. He could tell you."

Rein turned back to look at Eddy, "Oh, well I'll bet he couldn't tell you of a certain royal decree that Snow is trying to set you up for now could he?"

Edward shook his head, "What the hell are you talking about?"

"I'm talking about this stupid decree that her family has followed by tradition where she can only marry someone from a royal background, namely you Eddy. You're Prince Charming! God, can you believe that!" Rein laughed. "It's so blasted ironic, it's laughable. Not for Snow of course. Because that poor girl thinks she has no choice in the world for a husband but YOU. And that's the tragedy right there! She's so loyal to her family that she will put a blasted family tradition before true love. And with someone who would never want her, no doubt!"

"Well, now who said I would never want her?"

Rein pointed his finger, "Now don't even go there Ed. Don't even try and pull something like that over on her!"

Just then there came a painful scream from the bathroom. Edward and Rein went running in that direction. Once there, they found Mitch kneeling beside Snow, unconscious on the floor ... a small pool of blood under her neck.

"God, what happened!" Rein tried to approach her.

"We need the first aid kit now! Right now! Someone get some

bandages to stop her bleeding." Mitch was almost in a panic.

Kate joined him on the floor next to Snow having had Red Cross training, "She must have fainted, but her neck has been cut. Looks like just a nick. It missed her jugular, thank God! She wouldn't have had a chance without proper medical attention."

Tweety was sitting on the sink watching everyone.

"Wha' happened?" sobbed Stevie, crying at the site of Snow in such distress.

"What's that?" Donnie walked over to the wall and pulled out a shard of glass with blood on it, located at just about where Snow's neck would have been had she been standing. "This looks like a piece of a mirror. And it's got blood on it. How did it get here? It was just stuck into the wall 'ere ... what th' hell?"

Stevie cupped his hand over his mouth as he saw his broken mirror piece in Donnie's hand.

Chapter 8
"Mirror of Blood"

When Snow opened her eyes, she was in the guest bedroom in the main cabin. In the room with her were Stevie and Yolanda, and Tweety was sitting on the bedpost watching. She jolted up in the bed in a panic.

Yolanda gently put her hands on Snow's shoulders, "Snow, it's alright. You're with friends. You've had a rough episode, though."

Snow winced in pain as she touched her neck. She found a bandage wrapped gently around it and the pain from the cut smarted.

"Your neck was cut. We don't quite know what happened. We hoped you could shed some light on it. Donnie found a broken piece of a mirror jarred in the wall. It had blood on it. Did it cut you in some way?"

Snow thought back for a moment, then looked up at Tweety. It suddenly all came back to her and she gasped, "There was a mist ... like in the woods that day, Stevie, remember?"

Stevie frowned as he tried to remember.

A mist?" Yolanda looked at Snow quizzingly.

"Yes, and it began to swirl around the room. It scared me just like it did that day in the woods. Then I heard Tweety cry and as I turned to look at him, I felt a sharp pain in the side of my neck. I touched where it hurt and there was blood. That's all I remember before waking up here."

"Sounds like if you hadn't have turned, that mirror shard could have killed you, then. Kate said it nicked you very close to your main artery there," Yolanda directed to her neck.

"Aye, then it was Tweety who saved you! Saved by the bird, you were Snow!" Stevie picked up Tweety with his hands and held him.

Yolanda frowned, "Then Jill could be right. When Stevie told us about the mirror shard and where he found it, Jill thought maybe it was a piece of the queen's mirror ... meaning your step-mother, the queen ... the witch!"

"What! No, it couldn't be. You're scaring me. I'm in a totally different time and place now. She can't find me," gasped Snow.

Stevie touched her hand, "But Snow, you just said yourself about th' mist in th' woods, there. Ya saw it in the loo there too, right? That day in th' woods, I found that piece of mirror in the very spot I found ya, Snow." He began to tear up, "I feel s' guilty Snow. It's my fault. All of this is my fault!"

"Nonsense! Stop blaming yourself Stevie!" Yolanda looked into Snow's eyes as if she were going to ask her something very important, "Snow, did you ever overhear your stepmother speak to her mirror back home?"

Snow replied instinctively, "Yes, all the time."

Stevie and Yolanda looked at one another. "You don't think that's part of HER mirror do you?"

Snow gasped again. "How did she get here? What am I going to do? What's to become of me?" Snow grabbed Yolanda's arm and began sobbing uncontrollably.

"Calm down Snow. It's going to be alright. It was just a shard from a mirror. It probably just fell through the same portal, or whatever, that you did. I'm sure it's just a fluke. Donnie threw it into the fireplace. It won't come after you again. Now, you need to get some rest. Stevie will stay here with you and make sure you're not alone, OK?"

"OK, " Snow sniffed uncertain about everything. Yolanda smiled and closed the door as she left the bedroom. Snow took Tweety gently from Stevie and cradled him. "Looks like you're my bodyguard, little Tweety. Please stay by my side. You're like my guardian angel."

Stevie began to cry again, "Snow, it looks like I'm no good at guarding ya anymore, so ya need to keep yer bird. It's my fault all this 'appened."

"Stevie, no. Yolanda is right. It's not your fault. You didn't know. We just have to be really careful from now on regarding anything related to the woods. With all the strange things that have gone on, you just don't know anymore."

"Yeah, you're right, Snow. We gotta keep an eye out. But ya gotta rest now Snow. I promise this time I won't let anything 'appen to ya. Cross my heart, Snow." Stevie made a cross motion over his chest.

Snow smiled and patted his hand and rested Tweety beside her on her pillow. Even though the events of the evening were rushing through her head, sleep and Snow finally found each other.

As Yolanda came back into the main room, she was bombarded by Mitch and Eddy, "How is she?" Mitch managed to sputter.

"She's just gone back to sleep. It would be better if she didn't have any visitors for a while I think. She's had quite a scare."

"What was the story? What did she say happened?" Edward inquired, almost afraid to hear the answer.

Yolanda paused as she looked down, "It was just as we feared. There was a strange mist in the room she said, and then the shard flew at her and tried to kill her. If she hadn't moved just slightly the way she did, she'd be dead right now."

Donnie shook his head, "I know Stevie feels real guilty right now, but I do wish he'd 'ave told us about the mirror in th' woods."

"I guess I should have said something," Kristen cowered.

"What are ya talking 'bout, woman?" Donnie eyed her suspiciously.

"Well, the other day Snow told me about the mist in the woods and how it tried to choke her till she ran out of it and back to the village. I just thought she had an overactive imagination with all of this recent 'spooky woods' talk. That must have been when Stevie found the mirror. I guess what she told me really happened to her."

"Dammit woman! Why didn't ya say anything till now!" Donnie stood up from his chair near the fireplace.

"I just told you. I thought she imagined it!"

"Everything around here is important enough to mention no matter how small! Does everyone got that?" Donnie shouted as he looked around the room at everyone. The others nodded.

"Well this whole thing is just too creepy for me anymore, " shrugged Rein as he sipped his cider.

"Amen to that. I even let Yolanda take over the nursing duties for me." Kate spouted with a shudder.

"I don't get you people!!" flamed Eddy. "This innocent girl, a child almost, comes into this village. You all 'pretend' to be her friend and then one strange thing happens and you all turn on her! I don't get it! Weird things were happening around here long before she ever came here, remember?"

"That's not true Eddy. We're not all turning on..." Yolanda began but was quickly interrupted by Rein.

"Alright then, Your Majesty! Why don't you just take care of her then and save us all the trouble! 'Little Miss Innocent' in there ... the whole thing is starting to make me sick!"

Edward glared at him, "I don't EVER want to see you around her again! You got that, Partridge!!"

"Fine with me, 'Prince Charming'! I don't know about the rest of you, but I need a drink!"

As Rein exited into the kitchen, Duncan raised his hands, "Alright, that's enough of this. Look, we've all been through a lot tonight, and God knows that alcohol has played its role in the scheme of things. We all just need to calm down and get some rest, all right? Just like Jill and Donnie have said, strange things happen on Halloween and that's why we've all decided to stay here together tonight. This is probably just an isolated incident. I'm sure everything will be fine tomorrow."

"Well thank you for your enlightened words of wisdom,

Duncan, but how can you be so sure?" Mitch folded his arms.

"I'm not completely sure to be honest, but we've taken every precaution to be sure, Mitch. Alright? Now let's all get some sleep before we're all at each other's throats." He gave a quick glance at Yolanda, "Sorry, poor choice of words."

"Who's in with Snow right now?" Eddy approached Yolanda.

"Stevie is in there with her."

"Stevie! He the one that got her in this mess."

Donnie gave him a look.

"That's it. I'll just stay with her tonight, if it's all the same to you people." Edward headed for the bedroom.

Ivan watched him leave, "What's gotten into him all the sudden?"

Mitch never took his suspicious gaze off Edward, "I don't know, but I'd sure consider it one of the strange things happening around here. That's for sure."

"Stevie, wake up. I'm taking over Snow's watch."

Stevie rubbed his eyes and pretended to not have been asleep. "No, no. It's OK. I promised Snow that I'd..."

"Stevie, you can go now!" Eddy's voice was stern and Stevie knew he meant what he said.

"Well, you just better keep a good eye out, OK?"

"Don't worry, Stevie. She'll be fine."

Once Stevie was gone, Eddy brushed his hand through the sleeping princess' hair. "What have you done to me Snow? You're making me crazy. I used to know what I wanted. My desires were black and white, but now ... now everything is more like shades of grey. And you're there in the middle, Snow. You, this night, these strange events that they all seem to blame you for ... but I don't. You, just like the rest of us, are a victim in all of this. What do you really want, Snow? You don't really want someone so hardened as me, do you? Someone whose been around the block way too many times for you, Snow? You're almost untouchable, you know? Maybe not for someone like Stevie, but for me? Would you really want someone like me? I'm not really

'Prince Charming', Snow. But believe it or not, I'm willing to try, I suppose. If I'm able. Remember the archery contest? We have something in common there. And of course there's the royalty thing, which is apparently a bigger deal to you than it is to me, but nonetheless, there you have it. Oh, I don't know what I'm trying to say. I don't even know what I'm thinking. Ever since I got here to the village, I really haven't considered that a relationship with anyone was in my best interests, except for my brothers here in the Willows. Although, sometimes I do miss having a companion, but I just don't think I would know how to treat you. Don't you see? At least not treat you the way you're used to ... or rather the way you deserve to be treated. I'm used to having, what's the word, a plaything of sorts ... I guess you'd call it. And that's not you, Snow. You aren't a 'plaything', you're a Princess. Argh! I'm not saying any of this right. I'll just shut up. I'm glad you're asleep, Princess. Maybe one of these days I'll figure out what I'm trying to say and say it right."

Turned on her side, Snow faced the window, her eyes as big as saucers. She HAD heard what Edward said ... heard every word. Her heart pounded in her chest so loud that she was afraid Edward would hear. She felt those silly butterflies come to visit her again in her stomach and she wanted to swallow, but she didn't dare, for fear that he may see and know she was awake.

After about an hour, Ed began to feel his eyelids getting heavy. "You know, I'm going to get some coffee right quick like." Eddy peered out the door and saw Stevie sitting reading one of his books, while Ivan and Bart were outside on watch talking to Donnie. The others in the main room were finally asleep after a blowout earlier with Kristen, Donnie and Murray.

"Stevie, can you do me a favor?"

Stevie jumped up and rushed over to him, "Sure thing, Eddy. How's Snow?"

"She's fine. I wondered if you could just watch her door here while I get some coffee? But you don't have to go into the room. I don't want anything to wake her."

"Sure, Eddy. I can do that." Stevie sat back over in the corner and continued to read his book, glancing now and then in the direction of the bedroom. As Eddy walked into the kitchen, snoring could be heard in different parts of the room. The fire had died down to a dull flicker, barely lighting the room enough for Stevie to read by, but he was used to it. There was a light billow of smoke coming from the fire. Unnoticed by Stevie, the smoke drifted down to the floor and slowly began to flow toward the bedroom where Snow was sleeping.

Edward stepped out of the kitchen and witnessed the smoke cloud now making its way under the door.

Stevie, we have to get her out of there!"

Stevie jumped out of his chair now seeing the smoke traveling under Snow's door.

They both ran outside passing the men on watch, "'ere now, what's goin'on?" as Donnie and the other two followed them.

"We have another situation, men. Just come on!" They approached the window of the bedroom. Snow was still sleeping, and the cloud was now hovering over the bed just below the ceiling.

"Snow!"

She couldn't hear Edward yelling through the window, so he grabbed a large tree branch and crashed it through the window, startling Snow, who upon seeing the cloud above her ran toward the window. Edward had jumped through the window and grabbed Snow. Ivan helped him lift Snow through the window to safety outside. The cloud, swirling in anger above, lashed out and struck Edward knocking him down. It then vaporized and was gone. The men pulled Edward outside.

"Eddy? Eddy, are you alright? " Ivan shook Eddy, but he was unconscious.

Stevie touched Snow's arm, "It got 'im instead of you Snow!"

Snow kneeled down to him and wailed, "Not Edward ... No!"

"What the blazes is going on in here? Why is the window broken? Hello? Is anyone in here?" Kate went to the window followed by Kristen and Jill. "What is going here? We heard glass breaking. Why are you all outside?"

"It's a long story, Kate," Donnie muttered as he and the other men picked up Edward and carried him back around the cabin and into the main hall. They laid him down on the floor away from the fireplace.

"Alright, I need a canning jar and a cooking pan ... oh, and a heavy hammer or something I can crush this blasted mirror shard with. Here, give me those tongs." Donnie fished the mirror shard out of the fire with the tongs and placed it in the frying pan that Mitch brought in. Then with a meat tenderizer hammer, Donnie smashed the mirror shard several times until it was almost in a powder form. Mitch then poured the powder into a canning jar and sealed it in.

After a brief explanation of what happened from Stevie, Kate looked over at Snow who was sitting on the floor next to Edward, "Maybe you ARE cursed, Snow."

Tears welled up in her eyes and she looked down at Edward, still unconscious.

"Hey, can we refrain from name calling please! No one in here is cursed!" Mitch announced as he went to wash the pan in the kitchen.

Ivan picked up the jar and eyed its contents, "What do we do with the jar? We don't know that it's safe even bottled up in here."

Donnie took the jar in his hand, "No we don't. And first thing in the morning, we're taking it back to where Stevie found it. Maybe we can find a clue about what's going on here."

"I'm not going back to that place." Snow quivered as she spoke.

"Under the circumstances, I think that it would be best for you not to." Yolanda touched her shoulder to try and comfort the frightened girl.

Snow went into hysterics, "It's her! That witch! My step-mother did this to him ... is doing this to all of us!" She jumped up and grabbed the jar from Donnie and began to vigorously shake it, "Margurite! Leave my friends alone! I'm the one you want, you witch! Here I am! Come and get me! I'm not afraid of you! You hear me!! Come and GET ME!!"

Donnie grabbed the jar away from Snow, "God, she's flipped her lid!"

Mitch grabbed Snow and hugged her as she sobbed into his chest.

"Eddy! Look, he's awake." Kristen pointed down at Edward with his eyes wide open peering in the direction of Mitch and Snow.

Snow rushed over to him and dropped to the floor. "Edward, are you alright?"

She looked into his deep green eyes. Green? Edward sat straight up and grabbed Snow's shoulders. Snow gasped. He closed his eyes and grabbed his head as he lay back onto the floor, moaning. Snow was frozen.

Duncan knelt on the other side of Edward and gently shook him, "Eddy? Are you alright? Eddy?"

"Ow! What happened?" as Eddy rubbed his head where it hit the floor after the smoke cloud struck him.

"You were knocked out. Are you alright?"

Edward looked at Snow, "Yes, but are you alright Snow? There was smoke ... it was after you."

"Yeah, it's gone. We got that mirror shard in th' glass 'ere" Stevie pointed to the jar.

Snow was studying his face, his eyes. They were brown. But they were green a moment ago ... or were they? Was she imagining it? Did anyone else see it?

"How do you feel Edward? Do you feel anything ... strange?" Snow eyed him mysteriously.

"Strange? Why would I feel strange, except for this blasted headache I got now."

The men helped him to his feet. Duncan suggested they all get some more rest and stay together until the night was over.

"I have a feeling that this isn't the last we will see of the strange events." as Thomas looked at the jar that Donnie held in his hand and then at the front door of the cabin.

Chapter 9
"Don't It Make My Brown Eyes Green"

Snow laughed as she remembered Kristen's funny ghost story from the night before. She giggled even harder as she thought about the way Stevie jumped when Kristen lunged at him at the end of the story. The scary stories were something that Snow didn't mind remembering from the evening. However, there were certain events that she would just as soon forget, like the cloud above her bed or the mirror shard. She shivered as she touched the bandage still wrapped around her neck. Donnie and a few of the other men went to take the jar with the mirror's remains back to the forest. With Stevie leading them to the same spot he found Snow, she opted not to go back, as the girls thought that was best anyway. Snow's duties for the day found her cleaning in the barn and feeding the horses. Then her thoughts drifted back to the previous evening. As she petted the young colt, 24-Carrots, she remembered back to her conversation with Mitch, and of course ... their kiss. Even if just for that moment, it was like her life was complete. She remembered that his kiss matched his eyes, warm and tender. But what about Kate, she thought? What was this 'date' all about. She wanted to ask Kate but was afraid to. Kate had been rather 'stand-offish' since the events in the main cabin, and Snow didn't dare ask Mitch. And what was up with Rein? Why did he want to impersonate Edward? And how much of their conversation in the woods had he heard? How did he know about the decree? Did he eavesdrop on she and Yolanda as well? She began to worry about Edward. She hadn't seen or spoken with him since the night before, since she thought she saw him with those deep green eyes. Surely, she imagined that. As badly as she wanted to talk to Mitch, she decided to find Edward instead, at least to make sure he was feeling alright.

"Hey, I wondered if I might find you here, man. Trying for supper?" inquired Duncan as he came upon Edward fishing in the usual spot.

"Yeah, I suppose."

`"Hey, Eddy, what's the matter? You were acting very strange at breakfast. I don't think you said a word. And you look rather pale this morning. Are you all right?"

Edward rubbed his brown eyes, "Well, I don't know. Actually, I've felt rather strange ever since last night. But I'd rather you not tell anyone. I don't want to worry the others and I surely don't want the girls fussing over me. You know what I mean?"

Duncan chuckled, "Yes, I think I know just what you mean. I won't mention it. But if you're still feeling under the weather for too long, you need to let someone know, alright?"

Edward nodded. "Duncan, can I ask you something?"

"Certainly."

"Well, I know that you talk with Yolanda quite a bit, and, well ..." His voice trailed off and he looked into the water.

"Ed, what is it?"

"Well, I wanted to get your opinion on this whole 'decree thing'. You know ... with Snow?"
"My opinion on it how?"

Eddy continued, "Do you think she and I would ..." he hesitated, then quickly spat out "...make a good match?"

Eyebrows raised, "Well Edward, that's something you have to decide for yourself. But if I may say that this is rather surprising. In the past, you have always stated that you're done with relationships."

Edward gave an emphatic motion with his hands, "Exactly! That's right, but ... I don't know how to explain it. Ever since last night, it's almost like ... like something I really need to do, or rather ... oh I don't know. I can't explain it. It's just that I can't get the idea out of my head."

"What idea, Eddy? Marrying Snow?"

"Well, yes." He muttered almost under his breath, "Like voices in my head."

"Edward, it sounds like you're still feeling strange from the events of last night. I think you just need a few days to rest."

"I'm sure you're right. But maybe a companion would be good for me. What do you think, Duncan?"

"I'm thinking that catfish sounds like a fine idea for dinner, Eddy. Why don't you see what you can do?"

"Gotcha, Duncan."

"Why do I keep getting these dizzy spells? They're driving me crazy!" Edward sat down on a nearby stump. He was trying to shoot a few rounds of archery but could barely see the target with his recent sporadic blurred vision. Even though the spells had been going on a few days now, Eddy hadn't told anyone except for Duncan that first day.

Along with the spells, he also could not shake thoughts of Snow from his mind. What was it about her that had him so mesmerized recently? Ever since the party, he couldn't get her out of his head, nor shake the thought of her decree and a royal union out of his mind.

"Oh, hello. I wasn't expecting to find anyone here." Snow was surprised to see Edward by the archery targets. "I thought everyone would be all 'gamed out' now that the festival was over."

Edward smiled, "Oh no. I'll never tire of archery. How about yourself? Here to practice a few?"

"Yes, as a matter of fact. Could you please hold Tweety a second while I prepare my bow?"

"Of course." Edward took Tweety in his hands and began to pet him. Tweety sat happily within Edward's hand.

After a few rounds together, Snow offered "We haven't spoken since All Hallow's Eve, really. I wanted to make sure everything was all right after what happened. How are you feeling?"

"Oh yes, everything is fine. Thank you for being concerned. I've been ... fine." Edward paused for a second, "Well, actually that's not entirely true, Snow. I've actually been thinking a lot lately ... about everything. But mostly about you."

Surprised, Snow dropped the arrow that she was trying to load into her bow, "About me?"

"Yes. I know this will sound crazy, but ever since the party, I haven't been able to stop thinking about you, about your decree ... your royal union."

Snow set down her bow for fear she may drop it, too.

Edward continued, "What I'd like to do is perhaps ... get to know one another better, like when we go fishing, you know ... talk more. Explore the possibility of a union, a union between us."

This statement took Snow's breath away to where she almost couldn't breathe or speak. Finally, she managed "Edward, I would never try to suggest something that was against your better judgement..."

He interrupted Snow taking her hands in his, "I know that Snow, and this is all my idea, really. And if it is all the same to you, it would probably be better to keep this our little secret for a while, just until we can come to a final decision. You know how the others can be, especially the girls."

Snow smiled and nodded.

"They really look out for you, Snow ... like a little sister."

"Well, I think that since the festival, I've got them a little spooked, frankly." She paused and looked at the ground, hesitating, "Edward, does this mean that we're ... "

Eddy brushed her hair from her face, "Engaged? Well, that's up to you, Snow. Of course, I'll let you make that decision."

Snow turned and walked toward the target to get her arrows, "Well, if it's alright, I would like to think about it for a bit, since this is all happening very fast, and also with the rather strange things that have been happening lately."

While Snow's back was turned, Edward got one of his spells and had to sit back down on the trunk.

Tweety who was on a nearby branch, squawked and quickly flew away. "Don't take too long, my dear."

The sudden stern tone startled Snow. She turned back toward Edward to once again find those deep green eyes peering back at her. Not again! She was frozen with fear, just like the other night.

From the sky, Tweety swooped down and popped Edward in the back of the head, squawking. "Ouch!" He lowered his head to rub it and when he raised his eyes back to Snow, they were brown again. "Was that Tweety that just dive-bombed me?"

Snow took a step towards him, "What did you just say?"

"I said was that Tweety that just..."

"No, before that."

"Nothing. You had said you would like to think about it and I was just about to answer you. I was going to say, take all the time you want, Snow. I think it would be best for us to get to know each other. I want to get to know you, Princess."

Snow shook her head, "But you just said..."

"Aye, Snow! Whatcha doin'? Oh, 'allo, Eddy! Ya practicin' yer bow an' arrow shootin', there?"

Edward began to reload his bow, "Yes, Stevie. We were. Would you like to join us?"

Snow felt a sick feeling in the pit of her stomach. She needed some water. "I'm going to go on back. But you two please go on ahead. I'm just rather thirsty and need a glass of water. Thank you for the practice, Edward."

Snow was in a daze. Was she dreaming or had Edward just proposed, sort of? She hadn't used the Dixie Love Oil since the party, so she couldn't understand what was happening unless the potion was really that potent. And there were those green eyes again! She was still feeling sick to her stomach.

Snow hesitated before she walked around to the back door

of the kitchen. She wanted to get a cup of tea made from some of Jill's herbs to help settle her stomach. However, she was hoping against hope that Mitch wasn't in the kitchen. Just as she was about to enter, she heard laughing inside. She pressed her ear to the door. Although she detested eavesdropping lately, she couldn't resist. She heard Mitch in the kitchen with Kate laughing and carrying on. She didn't dare walk through that door now. Not wanting to be seen 'listening' at the door, she quickly hurried away.

'Fine', she thought. Then it was settled ... she would marry Edward. Why not? It didn't seem like Mitch would miss her company all that much, now. She went to Jill's cabin to gather some material for her dress. Of course, she would keep it secret as long as possible ... just as Edward had said. The others ... they just wouldn't understand. She would wait and tell them at the last possible moment. In the meantime, it would give her the time to make the preparations. There was only one thing left to do ... tell Edward.

As he crept up the ladder to the tree house, he tried to conceal the weapon he carried. Quietly and unnoticed by Snow, he opened the door. He found her sleeping on her couch pillows, having fallen asleep sewing a dress. He lowered the light in her lantern dimming the lighting of the room. Gently he knelt beside her, his green eyes twinkling with the reflection of the sharpened kitchen knife that he slowly brought to her throat. Suddenly, Tweety began squawking and flying around the sleeping princess. Snow's eyes fluttered as she awoke.

Edward quickly hid the knife, "Hello, Snow. I didn't mean to wake you."

Snow was surprised by his presence, but smiled nonetheless, "Hello Edward."

"I wanted to speak with you, Snow."

With the low light in the tree house, Snow didn't notice Edward's green eyes. "Yes, Edward. I wanted to talk to you, too. I've made my decision. I will marry you."

"Wonderful, my dear. I think the sooner, the better." She sleepily brushed her hair from her face.

"But I thought you wanted to take some time to get to know one another..."

"There will be plenty of time for that, dear. We could definitely use the time alone." He firmly took her face in his hand as he fidgeted with the knife in his other hand behind his back. "I'll arrange everything. It should be as soon as possible." Again, Tweety began squawking and fluttering about the tree house.
Snow was trying to calm him down, "I don't understand this. He's never done this. It's like the other day when he dive bombed you out of the blue, remember?"

Nervously, Edward started backing toward the door, "Yes, I do. Oh, well he probably just smells Jane's cat on me or something. That's all. I'll let you sleep, my dear. Goodbye."

Snow looked at Tweety, "Tweety, what's the matter with you? Did you have a bad dream or something? Rude bird! Wait ... Jane? Did he say 'Jane's cat'? Surely, he said Jill. I just heard him wrong."

Snow watched the door long after Edward left, thinking. That was very strange. She knew that she should have been happy, but all she felt was confused. He acted so ... different. Maybe he was just tired. But his touch was so cold, not like someone she would marry at all. It was almost ... controlling. It must have been just because he was tired. Nevertheless, she began working on her wedding dress again which she would continue to hide in her tree house.

It had been a long time since Snow had cooked, but she pretty well remembered the castle cook's famous recipe for stew. It was a rabbit stew, although after much argument from Snow, she had some of the men go out to catch some wild rabbits, as she refused to cook any animal she 'knew personally' ... as she put it. That afternoon before supper, Mitch offered to help her peel the vegetables. Snow was somewhat reluctant, as being around Mitch was difficult for her. But she accepted his offer. She just promised herself she would keep her betrothal in mind.

"So where did you learn to cook?"

"The castle cook, Amanda taught me. I remember her recipe for rabbit stew the best. By the way, thanks for talking the guys into catching the wild rabbits for me."

"Of course, Snow. I know how much you love the animals around here. Are you planning a dessert?"

"Oh of course ... gooseberry pie."

Mitch almost shouted, "You're famous gooseberry pie? What a treat we are all in for today!"

"Yes, it was Amanda's favorite, as well."

Mitch watched Snow peeling potatoes and snapping peas. No matter what activity she was involved in, she was so lovely ... with that air of innocence so uniquely hers. "You look so lovely today, Snow."

She blushed, "Oh, Mitch thank you, but I must look a mess, working in the kitchen all day."

Mitch took her hand, "If I had my way, you and I would be together like this every day."

Snow gulped and looked up nervously. Their eyes met for a moment as he rubbed her hand in his.

"Mitch, we should keep working or we will be serving dinner at midnight." Snow went to move the basket of potato peels closer to her to catch her droppings, but instead it started to fall over. She lunged to the floor to catch it. Mitch also lunged, acting like he was going for the basket as well, but instead grabbing Snow into his arms as she gasped quietly and started to get back up.

Mitch held her gently, and wouldn't let her, "Snow, I need to tell you this. Please hear me out. Ever since the party, and even before that you are always on my mind. No, I mean you are always on my heart. You are my heart, Snow. And I know that you think you have to follow this decree of yours, but you don't. Follow your heart, Snow." He softly touched her face and then her lips, "That night when we kissed, I know it came from your heart, Princess, as it did mine. Please listen to your heart now. I don't want you to feel uncomfortable around me, but I know why. We both know. Don't hold yourself back. We constantly engage in this petty chit-chat in order to keep from sharing our true feelings for one another. But I want us to share those feelings. Perhaps not here on the kitchen floor, but what about tonight? Can we talk later? At the tree house maybe? Please, Snow. I would really like to talk to you without this 'wall' between us."

Snow lowered her head. She couldn't look him in the eyes. She was already on the verge of tears. If she looked at him now, she knew she would break down and cry in his arms. As much as she wanted to do that, as much as she wanted to talk to him, share things with him, as much as she wanted him ... she couldn't. She knew that. Be strong, Snow. You have to tell him.

"Mitch, you don't understand. It's too late. I'm betrothed now. Edward and I have already discussed it. It's settled."

Mitch lifted her head so he could look into her eyes with his ... those warm brown eyes. She hoped that they would never turn green. However difficult, she was able to hold back her tears a little longer, "Snow, what are you saying? Are you telling me that you and Edward are engaged to be married already?"

Snow nodded.

"When did this happen?"

"Yesterday. He's making the arrangements. We were going to wait before we told anyone."

Mitch let go of her and sat back onto the floor. "Obviously. So no one else knows?"

Snow got up and sat back down in her chair, "Not that I know of yet."

Mitch came over to her and knelt beside her chair and took her hand, "Snow, you cannot marry someone unless you love him. Otherwise, you're just setting yourself up for a life of misery ... a life in hell."

"Don't try and scare me, Mitch. It won't work."

"I'm telling you the truth, Snow. Do you love him?"

"I have to get to work, Mitch. Why don't you just go. Dinner is my responsibility, tonight."

Mitch repeated the question in a sterner tone, "Do you love him?!"

The kitchen door opened and in walked Kristen and Yolanda. "Hey, there. Thought you all could use a hand?"

Snow smiled with relief at their entrance, "Yes, please. Kristen, could you please go with Mitch to the garden to get some more peas? I'm pretty sure we have a few more out there and I'm not sure I have enough for dinner."

"Sure thing. Come on, Mitch." Mitch frowned as he got up to go with Kristen.

Snow was careful not to look at him as he left.

"OK Snow, Mitch is gone. Now what's going on?"

Snow couldn't hide things from Yolanda. She seemed to be pretty in tune with anything bothering Snow.

"I'd really rather not talk about it." She couldn't hold it back any longer. She broke into tears.

"Oh honey, here." Yolanda handed her a clean kitchen towel nearby. "Please don't cry. What is it? Can't you tell me?" She took Snow in her arms quivering, sobbing. "Well, that's OK. You can tell me later, then."

"You're doing what?!" Duncan turned to Edward as they sat outside the cabin after dinner. "I don't think I heard you right, Eddy."

"No, you heard right. Snow and I are getting married."

Duncan couldn't believe his ears, "When?"

Edward directed his brown eyes down at his cup, "In two days."

Duncan's eyes widened even more, "Two days! Have you lost your mind? You two hardly know each other. And this 'decree thing' is ridiculous in this day and age. You know that. At least wait a little longer, man. Get to know each other better."

Edward nodded, "Well, we will. We will get to know each other."

Duncan added, "You know, I used to think that very same

thing ... that two people could just get married first and then get to know each other later. But being with Yolanda more and more, I've realized that it's much better in a marriage for a man and woman to get to know each other first, before they are married."

Edward wasn't really listening, "We will have plenty of time alone on the honeymoon with no distractions and no one around to disturb us. We just both feel that we need to do this."

Duncan shook his head, "Why right now?"

Edward looked up at the stars, "Well, I don't know, really."

Duncan was still in disbelief, "You don't know? Edward, let me ask you this. Do you love Snow?"

Eddy looked at him, "What sort of question is that?"

"An important one that I expect an answer to. Do you love her?"

Edward got up, "Duncan, I don't have to justify my marriage with Snow to you or anyone else. I'm going to get some more coffee."

As Edward opened the cabin door, Duncan added "Take some advice from me then. Don't ask Mitch for anything under the circumstances. He's likely to slug you when he finds out, you know."

The room was silent. You could hear a pin drop. Edward and Snow had just announced their wedding to everyone after dinner. Edward actually did the announcing, while Snow did not dare look in Mitch's direction.

Edward looked around the room expectantly, "Well? Isn't anyone going to congratulate us?"

"Congratulations," spat Nicholas.

"Yeah, way to go Snow 'n Eddy!" came Stevie's clueless but cheerful reply.

Kate gave a look over at Jill unnoticed by the betrothed couple.

Jill simply gave a shrug, "Well, like I said, it's her life."

Yolanda shook her head, "So that's why she was upset in

the kitchen ... why she wanted Mitch to leave. No wonder she wouldn't talk about it."

Kristen leaned over to Yolanda, "A secret engagement. Well, we know why they kept it secret. She knew we would try and talk her out of it."

Donnie put down his cup on the mantle, "OK, Your Majesty, riddle me this. How you gonna get married? We ain't got no preacher 'ere."

Edward waved his hand, "Everything's been taken care of. Don't worry about anything."

Being the closest in the room to Edward, Snow could see him out of the corner of her eye as he held her to his side. He was squeezing her awfully hard, she thought. As she started to look at him, she stopped. She was afraid of what she would see. No one else was close enough in such a dimly lit room to see it. She couldn't do it. She refused to spoil the evening by looking into his eyes ... his green eyes.

Yolanda fidgeted with a piece of ivy, "All right, the fact remains that Snow is marrying Eddy, and there doesn't seem to be much we can do. She wouldn't even talk to me. So, I suppose the best thing to do is to help her out and make her happy. We really need to be supportive no matter how we feel about it, alright?"

The others nodded. Yolanda was arranging some greenery into a bouquet for the wedding. In the morning, she would add flowers so it would be fresh for the wedding.

"How's her dress?" Jill asked.

Kate shook her head, "No one has seen it. Apparently she's been working on it herself. She's kept it hidden in her house. I suppose she was working on it before anyone knew of the wedding."

"Oh this is all so ridiculous!" Kristen threw the arrangement to the floor that she was making for the wedding. "How can you all sit there and let her go through with this?"

"She won't, Kristen. Don't worry." Jill's reply came cool and collected with no doubts. She hadn't even looked up from repairing one of the shoes she was going to wear tomorrow.

Kristen looked at Jill, "She won't? How do you know?"

"Because I just have a feelin', that's all. It's a bunch 'o strange things happenin' wit' Eddy, see. I can't quite place it, but somethin's goin' on and it ain't over yet."

Yolanda put down the ivy, "You're scaring me Jill, as usual. What are you talking about?"

Jill continued, "Can't say yet. Don't know, really. But it should prove interestin' to say th' least."

Kristen rolled her eyes, "Oh great! Here we go again with all the weird stuff around here."

Kate added, "And did you notice it always seems to revolve around Snow? The weird stuff, that is."

Yolanda gave her a look, "Give her a break, will ya? You haven't let up since the party."

Kate sighed, "You're right, I haven't. Sorry."

Stevie was about to knock on the cabin where the girls were talking.

"Pssst, Stevie?" Stevie turned to find Snow standing in the shadows near the side of the cabin. She was wearing her white cloak, the one from the party.

"Snow! Oi, what are ya doin' 'ere?"

"Shhh. Come here, Stevie." She spoke very softly, carefully. Stevie approached her. "Stevie, would you come and stay with me for a while, at my house. I don't want to be alone."

"Sure Snow, but what about Eddy? Wouldn't he want to keep ya company since you'll be gettin' married tomorrow?"

Snow thought quickly, "Well, it's bad luck to see the bride before the wedding. Let's not take chances."

When they reached the top of the tree house. Snow closed the door. "Can you at least stay till I fall asleep?"

"Snow, I can stay longer than that if ya want."

She smiled, "You're so sweet. Thank you." And she kissed him on the cheek. He blushed, and remembered how he had reacted at the party during the spin the bottle game when Snow kissed him ... when he became embarrassed and dashed out of the cabin to go on watch. He wouldn't do that again. He really did like it when Snow kissed him ... she was his good friend after all. Snow took her cloak and draped it on one of the pillows.

"Aye, I see Mitch did a good job of washing the stain out of yer cape, there. I'm really glad. I thought I'd stained it for life. I felt really bad about that, Snow."

Snow had been battling her emotions all day, then to hear Stevie mention Mitch was just too much for her. She sank to the floor and began to cry into one of her couch pillows.

"Snow, I'm sorry. I didn't mean ta make ya cry. What'd I say? Snow?" He hesitantly put his hand on her shoulder.

She turned into him and hugged him, crying into his chest.

Stevie's eyes showed much surprise, "Snow, what's wrong?"

Snow's voice was muffled, "Nothing's wrong Stevie. Please don't talk, just hold me for a while, OK?"
"OK, Snow."

Snow was in need of an unconditional love that night. She didn't want Mitch's affections, nor did she want the responsibility of Edward's company. What she needed then and there was Stevie. His innocence coupled with her own ... his sincere affection and unconditional companionship were what Snow desperately needed. As he held her, he stroked her hair. He loved her soft hair. He stayed there with her until she fell asleep, until they both fell asleep.

Chapter 10
"Princes and Flowers and Bears, Oh My!"

"Well, how do I look?" Snow spun around in her white wedding dress in the orchard while Mitch was gathering baskets.

The dress was lovely, made with white silk and chiffon, much like her dress for All Hallow's Eve ... except this one was full-length. She even used her original flower crown again with new fresh flowers and a chiffon veil instead of ribbons. She thought it fitting to have her veil made from the same crown she had worn the night that Edward had first noticed her.

"Oh, Snow. You look ... you look beautiful." He tried to be cheerful and continued, "I've been stirring the mix for the wedding cake. It's going to be delicious..."

"Mitch," Snow interrupted, "Please, I don't want you to make us a cake. In fact, I ... I don't want you to be there today ... at the wedding."

"You don't want me to go to your wedding ... why?"

Snow closed her eyes to try and hold back her tears, "I think we both know why, that it would be too hard for both of us. I just think it would be best."

"Snow, look at you! You're miserable! Your wedding day is supposed to be the happiest day of your life, yet you are the most unhappy bride I've ever seen." Mitch put his hands on her shoulders, "Don't do this, Snow. Don't marry someone that you do not love with all of your heart, someone who isn't your 'true love'."

Snow pulled away and turned from him, "Please understand, Mitch. I have to do this. It's for my..."

Mitch didn't let her finish, "What, your family? Your kingdom? Your father? I know it isn't for your stepmother!"

"Mitch, you just don't understand..."

"No, I don't understand! I don't understand who it is you are trying to please. Who do you owe this great favor to? There isn't anyone around you Snow, but us. There are no members of your kingdom here to judge you. Please don't do this. I love you too much to see you make a mistake like this. I love you! You hear me, Snow? I love you! Don't go through with this."

In hearing this, her tears began to freely flow. He said he loved her! Snow couldn't turn and face him now, not now. She couldn't let him see her tears, her pain, "I'm sorry Mitch, but I must." Without saying goodbye, Snow ran out of the orchard.

Stevie walked with Snow to the clearing in the woods where the wedding was to be held. Snow gasped, "My bouquet! Stevie I forgot it, the one Yolanda made me. I have to have it. I know I'll be late, but I have to go back and get it."

"Don't worry Snow, I'll go back an' get it for ya! You go on ahead an' join th' others. Ya can't be out in these woods alone, ya know."

"Thank you Stevie. You're such a dear!"

As Stevie ran back to get her flowers, Snow began to walk toward the clearing. She began thinking to herself ... thinking about Edward, thinking about those strange green eyes. Is it really her imagination? Something strange about it though, was that there was something familiar about those green eyes, but she just couldn't put her finger on it.

She thought about Mitch. He said he loved her. No, don't think about Mitch. Am I doing the right thing, though? I do love Edward ... but do I love Mitch more? Oh Snow, stop it. It doesn't matter. This is your wedding day, the day you've always dreamed of. My duty will be fulfilled according to the decree, and of course I'll have my prince ... the prince in my dreams. Now cheer up. It was hard for Snow to muster a smile while she thought of Mitch's broken heart. But she was approaching the clearing and managed to conjure a smile.

As she drew closer to the clearing, Tweety began to squawk and flutter on her shoulder. "Tweety? What's the matter? What's wrong?" Suddenly, Tweety flew from her shoulder and into the woods away from the clearing. "Tweety!" She chased after him through the brush and trees. She could still hear him, but he wouldn't stop. "Tweety, stop! This is going to ruin my dress, you silly bird! What's wrong with you?"

Finally, she chased him to the river. There he was perched on some rocks that jutted out over the water. She crawled up onto the rocks to the edge overlooking the water and took the little bird in her hand. "Tweety, you naughty thing! What's wrong? You don't want me to marry Edward, do you? You've been acting strangely around him lately, why? Do you know something I don't know? I wish you could tell me." Something in the water below caught Snow's eye. She peered down and saw her reflection. Suddenly, it began to change. She found herself looking at a reflection of ... her father? "Daddy? Daddy, is that you?"

The reflection spoke back to her as clear as if he were standing in front of her, "Hello my little Princess."

"Daddy!" She reached down to the water, but she was too high up to touch the surface.

"Princess, you look so lovely ... and yet you are so sad, my child. I want you to do something for me. Will you?"

Snow smiled as the tears streamed down her face, "Of course, Daddy!"

"Princess, I loved you with all of my heart. All I ever wanted for you was to be happy. I want you to forget about the decree. I want you to find your 'true love'."

Snow sniffed, "Forget about the decree, Daddy? But.."

"You deserve to be happy, Snow, and not to have to worry about a set of staunch rules. Find true love, Snow. Can you do that for me?"

"If that is your wish, Daddy ... of course, I'll be more than happy to do that."

"Snow, always remember that I love you, and I'm watching over you, Princess. Goodbye!"

"Daddy, no! Don't go, please! Come back! I love you, too!" She suddenly remembered, "Wait Daddy! What about the queen, Daddy? She's after me. What do I do about Margurite?"

⚘ But there was silence in the water, and the reflection was now her own. As one of her tears made ripples in the water below, softly she whispered "Goodbye, Daddy." She lowered her head and buried her face in her hands.

She began thinking about her favorite things she used to do with her father. She remembered back to the time he taught her to dance and to shoot a bow and arrow. He called her a 'natural'.

Suddenly, her memories were interrupted. Tweety began to squawk and flew off of Snow's shoulder once again. "Tweety, what is it?" Snow heard a rustling in the brush in the distance, "Stevie, is that you? Edward? Anyone?"

She gulped and slowly climbed down from the rocks back to the riverbank. Out of the brush ahead came a shadow. As it moved further out of the brush, Snow was able to make out what it was. Oh God, it was a bear!! Without even a breath, Snow dashed back into the woods. The bear saw her and took off after her. She ran as fast as could, stomping through leaves and shoving away stray branches. With the brush tugging at her dress, it slowed her down and the bear got right on her heels. He lunged at Snow, but only ended up grabbing her veil in his teeth, pulling the flower crown off of her head. She kept running as fast as she could. Then she saw it. A perfect climbing tree ... her only chance. She sprinted up the tree as fast as she could ... probably faster than she'd ever climbed a tree in her life. She went as high as the branches would let her. When she looked down, the bear was at the foot of the tree, trying to lunge upward towards her. Snow was so scared, more scared than she had ever been. She did not take her eyes off of the bear. With her wedding veil in the bear's mouth, she watched it circle the tree and lie down at the foot of it.

It must have lied there for hours, or so it seemed to Snow. Finally, she saw it catch a rabbit and begin to devour it right on top of the chiffon, smearing blood all over the beautiful veil she had made. The sight repulsed Snow. She felt her stomach churn, and for once in her life would welcome those all too familiar butterflies right now. But they weren't there ... just a sick feeling in the pit of her stomach. After an eternity, the bear finally gave up on the entrée in the tree and left with Snow's veil still in its mouth. With mixed feelings of pure terror and relief, Snow began to cry up in that tree ... the tree that had just saved her life.

"Alright, what time was this wedding supposed to start again?" asked Trent as he looked at his watch. "Did they say 2:00 or 3:00?"

Kristen frowned and shook her head, "No, there's something not right here. They should be here by now."

"Here, I got it, Snow!" Stevie came rushing up, out of breath, holding a bouquet of flowers in his hand.

"Snow isn't here. She was supposed to be with you, Stevie? Where is she?" Kristen put her hands on her hips as she glared at Stevie.

"She forgot 'er bouquet an' I told 'er I'd go get it for 'er an' that she would come on over to th' clearing where you were."

Donnie approached Stevie, "Well, Stevie, she never made it. What have I told you about these woods? You know better! You can't leave anyone alone, especially Snow with her track record 'ere lately!" Stevie lowered his head and nodded. Donnie continued, "Alright, we need to create four search teams and search the woods. Let's pray we find her before it gets dark."

When Snow opened her eyes, it was just turning dusk. It concerned her that it was starting to get dark, but it concerned her more that the bear may still be down there waiting for her. She knew bears hunted more at night. She noticed that Tweety was safe and sound perched on her shoulder sound asleep. She realized that she must have fallen asleep in the tree, as she had done many times growing up. What could she do, though? She had to stay in the tree till morning ... in the darkness of the woods. She decided to take her chances with the darkness everyone spoke of rather than risk running into her bear 'friend' again. As the air grew darker and darker the shadows fell in a spooky way. They seemed to creep in on her ... closer, closer. Something suddenly caught her eye. She looked down at her family crest that she had pinned to the neckline of her wedding gown. It was glowing! Of course, then she remembered ... 'Daddy! He said he'd be watching over me. The darkness in the woods can't touch me with a glowing crest, right?' And so it was. The eerie darkness laid not a hand on the little princess as she slept through the night in the safety of the large tree.

⚘ Mitch was fixing dinner that evening for the village. He knew that Snow did not want him to come to the wedding. He didn't want to go himself. He thought about her in her beautiful dress and crown veil and again wished that ... argh! I need to not think about it and concentrate on dinner, he thought. He didn't want to think about it, about her, about them.

Harboring no hard feelings, he knew that Snow and Edward were to have a picnic dinner in her tree house to start off their honeymoon, and he went ahead and made them a small wedding cake and left it for them in the tree house. Come to think of it, the wedding was hours ago and everyone else should have returned for dinner by now. That's strange. Where is everyone still? It's beginning to get dark. Mitch began to take off his apron as he saw everyone coming back into the village from the woods. Something didn't look right, not right at all.

He approached the group heading into the main dining hall. "Is there something wrong?"

Stevie was crying, "Mitch, it's all my fault! I went back to fetch Snow's bouquet an' she said she was going to go on ahead to the weddin', but she never made it! We never found her! We looked and looked! All we found was this!"

He pointed to the object Kate was holding. Sadly, she presented Mitch with Snow's flower crown wedding veil covered in blood.

Mitch gasped, "God! We have to go look for her."

As he started off with the veil, Donnie grabbed his arm, "We've looked all afternoon. You know we can't go back till mornin'. You know that!"

Mitch pulled away from Donnie's grasp, "What I know is that Snow is out there and she could be hurt and in need of our help, especially in the dark!"

"We won't be helping her by getting ourselves killed out there, Mitch! Now back down!"

"No, I won't leave her out there, man. I won't!" Mitch started to take off but was caught by Donnie and Duncan.

As he struggled, Donnie looked at Duncan, "I think th' only way to settle him down is a night in jail. What do ya think?" Duncan nodded sadly and the men helped to drag Mitch off to the jail.

As they passed by Edward, Mitch lunged at him, "This is all your fault! You never loved her! You tricked her! Why can't you just leave her alone?" He got in a fairly good punch before Donnie and the others could get Mitch up off of him.

Taken by surprise, Eddy was helped back up by Kristen and Murray, "What was that about?" as he rubbed his jaw, now throbbing from Mitch's blow.

Once they got Mitch to the jail, Donnie locked him up, "Look, mate. We'll get out some more search parties first thing in th' mornin'."

Mitch clenched his teeth, "By then it might be too late! You know that! You don't care about her like I do!"

Donnie tossed the keys to Nicholas who agreed to stay with him for the night, "Here. See if ya can talk some sense into him."

It's light. It must be morning! As she opened her eyes Snow

thought, despite all the warnings, 'I survived the night in the woods.' She lifted her crest to her lips that was pinned to her wedding dress and kissed it, "Thank you, Daddy!" She looked around down below. No sign of the bear, but no sign of Tweety, either. "Tweety! Where are you? Oh!" Tweety landed safely on her shoulder and surprised Snow. "We have to get going. I know they are probably worried about me!"

As she climbed down the tree, the thought crossed her mind that she had missed her own wedding. But wait, Daddy released me from the decree yesterday, didn't he? I didn't dream that, did I? As she walked back to the village, she questioned her love for Edward ... no there really was no question. Although she was fond of Edward, she didn't love him, not enough to marry him. 'Find true love' ... these words from her father played over and over again in her mind. Snow had been raised in a society full of rules and others telling her what to do and how to do it. She was so used to this ... and now she was to make her own choices for love and marriage. The thought almost frightened Snow. She had always been surrounded by this wall of 'directions' ... but now, she had to make decisions on her own ... figure out life by herself. Would she do the right thing, Snow thought? Was she capable of making the right decisions? She'd followed her head for so long ... and now she had to follow her heart. She remembered those very same words from Mitch, 'follow your heart'. But the heart is such a complicated thing. She was afraid she could get so carried away, she would make the wrong choices. What should she do? With every thought, Snow came back to Mitch's words ... 'follow your heart'. She could see his face, his warm smile, his loving eyes ... brown eyes. Her steps became quicker and quicker until she was in a full sprint toward the village.

There it was ... the edge of the village, but there was no one around. She dropped to the ground just to catch her breath. She had run so fast, she was panting and wheezing. Where was everyone? Were they out looking for her? She hadn't heard any-one calling her name. In the distance she could see the main cabin. Perhaps everyone was there having breakfast. She was already so exhausted, she just wanted to sit there for a while, but she had to get to the cabin. She had to tell the others what happened ... how her father saved her in the woods. Slowly, she got up and started toward the hut.

Everyone was gathered in the main cabin. Donnie had set up the different search parties and was going over the plan of action. Mitch wasn't hearing any of it. Standing by the door and lost in his own thoughts, he grasped Snow's veil in his hand. He wouldn't let go of it. It was possibly the last thing of her. He just knew it was too late. He'd never forgive them for this ... for locking him up ... for keeping him from going after her.

And there was Edward. Mitch glared at him, but Edward didn't notice as he listened to Donnie's instructions, still wallowing in his own confusion over the whole situation. There were so many times during the last few days that he couldn't even remember. There were many moments that were fuzzy to him. He knew that he would have to tell someone soon. Could he have a concussion? He wasn't sure, but he brushed these thoughts away as he came back to Donnie's instructions.

Kate could tell how upset Mitch was as she looked on him with concern. She wanted desperately to speak with him last night in the jail, but Donnie had said he was too angry and probably wouldn't make much sense. She wondered how much of that was true and how much was Donnie just not wanting her to talk to him.

Mitch leaned his head back against the wood wall. Morning had fully broken now, as he peered out the window. "God!" He threw open the door forcefully and sprinted out with purpose.

"What the?" Donnie looked in the direction of the door to merely see it swinging open.

Kate ran to the door, "It's her! Oh God, it's her! She's alive!!"

Never had such a sight beheld Mitch's eyes than to see the Princess alive as he saw her heading toward the cabin through the window. He didn't even feel the veil drop to the ground nor feel the ground under his feet as he flew across the path to meet her. Snow found her ability to sprint return to her as she rushed towards him ... the words 'follow your heart' still resounding in her ears.

"Snow!" he twirled her off her feet ... around and around before both of them dropped to their knees on the ground. Both in tears, Mitch took her face in his hands, "Snow, you're alive! Princess..."

Snow smiled as she choked out a laugh. With her face still in his hands, Mitch gave her many short kisses until her muffled words stopped him, "In the woods ... it was my father. Mitch, he saved my life. I saw him! It was really him!"

Mitch smiled, not quite understanding her meaning, then grabbed her and hugged her tightly.

"Snow! It's really you!" came Stevie's sobbing voice from behind. "I didn't mean ta leave ya, Snow. I thought you'd go right to th' clearing, I did. You're alright! I'm s' glad you're alright!" He also dropped to his knees on the ground and hugged Snow on top of Mitch holding her.

The others came rushing over, led by Kate and Kristen.

Kate, still surprised, could hardly find the words, "How on earth? The woods ... how did you make it, Snow?"

Donnie was also speechless.

Kristen helped Snow to her feet with the aid of Mitch, "Let's all go in. I'm sure Snow has a lot to tell us. And I know I want a front row seat for this story!"

With the exception of the part about the decree, Snow told every second of her adventure in detail ... Tweety flying away, her father in the river's reflection telling her he would protect her ... and of course the bear.

Some were amazed and some were skeptical. Among the skeptical was of course Donnie. "I dunno. Sounds like it would more likely be one of our usual strange occurrences 'round 'ere rather than your father's ghost, or whatever."

"Oh, no. It was him. I know my father, and that was him ... no question."

"Well, maybe no question to you, Snow".

Donnie was always the paranoid one, Snow thought. But they don't understand. She KNEW that was her father ... no doubt about it. "But he protected me in the woods. There is no other way to explain that, Donnie."

"Well, I guess you can believe whatever ya want. But you were just damn lucky. That's all I gotta say 'bout it. You don't be doing that ever again. I don't care if yer blasted bird's being shredded to bits, you just don't do it!! You got it?"

"Yes, Donnie. I got it."

Donnie rubbed his forehead, "Man, I feel like a broken record 'ere ... am I? Cause I know I've given this speech before ... either that or I'm goin' crazy!"

Kristen raised her eyebrows, "No comment."

Donnie pretended not to hear her despite the quiet chuckles around the room.

Snow stood up and began to head toward the front door, "If you all don't mind, I need a word with Edward, please, alone. Edward, may we?"

Mitch felt his heart drop into his stomach as he saw Snow and Edward retire outside. 'To rearrange the wedding, no doubt, 'Mitch thought. Kate started over to talk to him, but he slipped into the kitchen too quickly. He wanted to be alone for a while.

"I think he'd rather not be disturbed right now, eh?" Donnie had witnessed the scene as he approached Kate. Tired of Donnie always trying to keep her from talking to her friend, she turned away and went to talk to Jill instead. Besides, she wanted to hear any kind of enlightenment she might have on this whole ordeal. Kate knew Jill would have some kind of opinion.

Chapter 11
"Possession"

Kate peered into the kitchen to check on Mitch, "Are you alright?"

"Yes Kate, thank you. I'll be alright."

"Do you want to talk about it?"

"No, not really. I mean, maybe later. I'm sorry, Kate. I don't mean to be rude."

"It's OK, Mitch. I understand."

Kate left the kitchen and went back in to talk with Jill and Kristen. Just as Kate thought, Jill said she knew Snow was alive and that she was OK. She regretted not telling Mitch, but figured he wouldn't have believed her anyway.

In the main door came Snow, alone. Since most eyes were on her at that moment, she felt like she had to offer an explanation, "Edward said he wasn't feeling well and went on home to lie down."

Duncan was concerned about his strange behavior the past few days and what Edward had told him the day after the party. He knew that Eddy was holding back something. "I'm going to check on him," as he went out the door.

Mitch's back was turned to the door when he heard it open and then close again. The room was silent even after the person's entrance. It must be Kate. He appreciated her concern, but was afraid he wouldn't be much for company tonight, "I'd rather be alone for a little while, if you don't mind Kate."

"I'm not Kate."

Mitch whirled around at the sound of the soft voice to find

her standing there. She was so beautiful in her white dress, even though a little tattered from her adventures in the woods. His voice quivered a little, "Snow, I thought you were talking to Edward."

"I was. And now I'm talking to you." Her tone was so confident, it made Mitch even more nervous. "Mitch, I haven't yet had the chance to tell you what my father told me in the woods."

"But you told everyone, I thought? Just now."

"No, this is something I didn't mention because I wanted to tell you first. Well, I actually had to tell Edward first."

Mitch lowered his gaze upon hearing Eddy's name.

"It was only for courtesy's sake, considering I was breaking our engagement over it."

He quickly caught her gaze once more with a questioning look, "Breaking the engagement? So you're not marrying Edward?"

Snow smiled, "No, I'm not."

Mitch was speechless as he could hardly breathe much less speak.

"The most important thing my father said to me was that he loved me very much and wanted me to be happy more than anything else. He said I shouldn't be worried about following any staunch rules, or what have you. He said I deserve to be happy and that I should find 'true love'. With that, he released me from the decree."

At that point, it was Mitch who began to feel the butterflies that so often graced Snow with their presence.

"So you see Mitch, I have to do just what you said, now. I have to follow my heart." Snow began to feel a lump in her throat and tears began to well up in her eyes as she turned slightly away and walked toward the counter. "I'm not quite sure how to do that, you know. I've had to follow the directions of others for so long. I've been following my head. The heart is a complicated thing, whereas following directions was so easy. I just want to be sure that I do the right thing. I don't know if I should follow my heart. I haven't had much practice." Snow wiped the tears from her face, she was annoyed that they were there.

Mitch approached her and gently put his hand on her shoulder, "Actually, you look like you'd be a natural at it to me, Snow."

She turned to look at him and smiled, "I know this will sound strange coming from a girl in her wedding dress, but it occurred to me that we've never even been on a date."

With boldness overcoming butterflies, Mitch stepped right up to Snow, put his hand around her waist and his other hand under her cheek, "Where would you like to go, Princess? The world is yours ... well, at least the village."

Snow put her hand on top of his resting on her cheek, "As long as you're there, that's good enough for me."

Then, he kissed her as he did that night of All Hallow's Eve.

Snow, responding to his kiss, had no convictions now. She was no longer betrothed, nor did she have a decree to concern herself with.

" 'ere ya are Snow. I've been lookin' for ya."

Once again their kiss was interrupted by an 'intruder' into the kitchen, but this time it was the cheery tone of Stevie. "They all wanted me to come ask you 'bout breakfast, Mitch. Not sure why they asked me, though. So how 'bout it?"

"Ah, of course, Stevie. I forgot." He turned to Snow, "You see, originally everyone made up sack breakfasts of fruit and muffins to take on the search for you this morning. Well, I guess now everyone is looking more toward a hot one, looks like. OK Stevie. Tell them I'll get started on something right away."

As Stevie left, Mitch began getting out some eggs and Snow stopped him by touching his arm, "Mitch, you're always such a dear, cooking for everyone. Why don't you get someone else to do it this morning? After all you made all those sack breakfasts for everyone."

Mitch lowered his eyes to the floor, "No, actually I didn't make the sack breakfasts, Snow. Kristen and Jill made them for me. I was ... I was in the jail."

Snow let go of his arm, "In the jail?"

Embarrassed, Mitch looked back at Snow, "Yes, they had to

lock me up because I wanted to search for you last night even though it was dark. I was going to go out alone, if I had to. So they locked me up to keep me from going."

Snow just looked into his eyes, not quite knowing what to say.

"You see Snow, they brought back your veil covered in blood, and I didn't know what happened to you, Princess. I thought you were ... well, I had to try to find you. I knew you were in danger. I was so angry last night ... at them. They had to lock me up, or I guess they thought they had to. It was the longest night of my life, though ... wondering where you were, if you were hurt, if you were still alive." He stopped, afraid he would choke if he spoke about it any more.

Snow could read it in his eyes. He was going to risk everything, including his own life, to search for her. She felt her love for him bubble up inside her and virtually explode. She couldn't help herself. Although uncharacteristic for her, she wrapped her arms around Mitch's neck and kissed him lovingly. Mitch willingly kissed her back wrapping his arms around her in return.

Suddenly, there was a knock at the kitchen door, "Mitch? You need any help in there?" It was Yolanda's voice. She knew Mitch and Snow were in the kitchen, so she didn't want to just burst in, but she also wanted to make sure they didn't need any help with the cooking.

Snow giggled. Mitch rolled his eyes, "Sure, Yolanda. That would be great ... but in just a minute." He looked at Snow. "This is getting old, constantly being interrupted every time that ...." He stopped. "You know what? It's this kitchen. It seems to be the most popular place in Whispering Willows. What about that date? Where do you want to go, just the two of us?"

Snow smiled flirtatiously, "Why don't you surprise me, Mitch. I'm sure I'll be delighted with anything you do." They looked at each other for a moment, "Why don't I help you with the breakfast, Mitch?"

"Oh, Princess, no. You have had way too rough of a night. In fact you should probably get some rest after breakfast. Just send

Yolanda in here and go on in and sit down and rest, OK?"

"Alright, Mitch." Snow sent in Yolanda and went back to sit with the other girls.

"OK, Snow. We now know why you've been so quiet lately keeping this big secret. So now ya better start talkin'. We wanna hear all about it, girl!" Jill was bold and inquisitive.

Snow told them about everything her father said in the woods and that she wasn't marrying Edward. She told them how it all came about. Snow pondered as she thought back, "It was all very strange at times."

Kristen raised her hands, "Wait a minute! Did you say that Eddy's eyes were green? You must have imagined it, honey."

"That's what I thought, but it happened more than once, and it was very strange ... he wasn't himself, really. And Tweety acted very odd around him during those times as well, come to think of it."

Jill put her hand on Snow's, "Snow, tell me exactly what he said and how he acted when ya saw him with th' green eyes."

"Well, his demeanor was different. He was ... colder. Plus, I suppose he seemed a little rougher than usual. At one point he took my chin in his hand, rather tightly ... not an action typical for Edward since I've been around him."

Jill took Snow's hand with both of hers and leaned in towards her, "Alright, I'm gonna ask ya a few questions that may scare ya ... but just bear with me, K?"

Snow looked at Jill confused, "OK."

"Now remember when ya were cut with that mirror shard? Yolanda said you an' Stevie talked about the possibility of th' attack coming from Margurite."

"Yes, I remember, but the men took that shard away to the woods in a jar after Donnie broke it."

"But before that, the shard was in th' fireplace and caused a smoke cloud that came into your room. When Edward lifted ya outside, th' cloud struck him, then disappeared."

Snow gulped. Surely, Jill wasn't suggesting ...

"Snow, when was th' first time ya saw Eddy with green eyes?"

Snow put her hand to her mouth, "Right after he woke up."

"An' Snow, what color are your stepmother's eyes?"

Snow began crying burying her face in her hands, "They're green, oh no! What have I done? And Edward would sometimes call me 'dear'. Margurite called me 'dear'. Jill, I've brought her with me! I've put the village in danger!"

Jill and Kristen stroked Snow's hair while Kate sat wide eyed at the thought.

Kristen leaned in to Jill, "Are you sure about this?"

"Yeah, I've heard legends 'bout people taking th' eye color o' their possessor, but I always thought it was jus' that ... legend. I guess there's some truth to it. But then again, look where we are." Jill turned back to try and calm Snow down, "Shhh, it's OK. We don't want to alarm the others. We don't need them to know jus' yet. We'll figure this out, Snow."

"Too late, there Jill." Donnie had overheard regardless. "Great, so ya brought yer stepwitch back with ya, did ya?"

Snow looked up at Donnie horrified.

"Gee, Princess. Thanks so much for the lovely gift!"

"Can it Donnie!" yelled Kristen forcefully. "She's been through enough without you shooting off your mouth!"

But Donnie continued, "So that makes Eddy 'the queen'! Pretty fittin', when ya think about it."

Kristen wished Duncan were here to shush up Donnie. Where was Duncan? "Wait, didn't Duncan go to Eddy's to check on him? He went to Eddy's alone!"

"That's it, men. Let's go." Donnie was out the door before another word was said.

"Hey, what's going on?" Yolanda rushed out of the kitchen followed by Mitch when she heard the shouting. She was afraid it was a repeat performance of All Hallow's Eve.

Kate looked at Jill as she got up. We have to tell Yolanda that Duncan is possibly in danger, thought Kate.

"Let me handle this one, girls. Yolanda, can I speak with you for a moment in the kitchen?"

Jill took Yolanda into the kitchen as Mitch came over to see why Snow looked so upset and crouched down to her.

Snow began sobbing again, "Oh Mitch, it's her! And Edward! I've brought her to the village somehow! I've put everyone in danger ... Edward, now Duncan!"

He touched her face, "Snow, what danger?"

"Margurite! She's taken over Edward. Green eyes! She's here!" Snow put her arms around Mitch's neck and buried her face in his chest, sobbing. Mitch, confused, looked at Kate. She nodded.

He pulled Snow off of the chair and down to the floor so he could cradle her, "It's OK, Snow. We won't let anything bad happen."

The worried look on Kate's face concerned Mitch. There really was something very wrong, wasn't there?

"On three! One-two-three!" At Donnie's command, he, Murray, and Ivan broke the door down at Eddy's hut, taking Duncan and Eddy completely by surprise.

Duncan jumped up, "What is going on?!"

Edward was sitting near the fireplace, still not feeling his best, "Good God, man! You could have knocked!"

Donnie ignored their inquiries, "Are you both alright?"

"Yes, what the devil is going on?"

Donnie walked toward Edward, "We need to lock Eddy up. Sorry, man."

"What did I do?"

"Nothing. It isn't you. It's that Margaret woman."

"Margurite," Ivan corrected.

"Whatever. Let's go."

As Donnie pulled Edward up by the arm, Duncan stepped in, "Wait a minute! No one is going anywhere till you tell us what's going on?"

Donnie and Ivan told them about Jill's theory on Snow's stepmother and the surrounding circumstances that Snow observed.

Eddy's jaw dropped. He was speechless, and scared. "Maybe

that's why I haven't been feeling myself lately. I get blackouts, things I can't remember ... plus the dizzy spells."

"Well, we can't take any chances. We gotta lock you up. I hope you understand."

Edward nodded at Donnie's precaution.

"But he isn't well, Donnie." Duncan continued, "That jail is no place for one who is sick, no matter the reason. He's our brother, man. Surely, there's another way. Why is the jail always your sole conclusion?"

"No, Duncan, it's OK. Donnie's right. I don't want anything else to happen. It's obvious I can't control what happens when I blackout, or whatever. To tell you the truth, the past few days have really been a blur. Except for a few occasions, I don't even remember talking with Snow about the wedding or making the arrangements. It just ... happened. I guess maybe it was that woman."

This all really scared Eddy, to not be in control of his own body. It terrified him. He didn't want anyone to get hurt. "Snow broke our engagement tonight. Under the circumstances, I think it was the best thing." Edward had mixed feelings on the issue. He still didn't know how he felt about Snow, but he knew that he didn't want anything to happen to her. And until this issue was settled somehow, he was going to keep his distance from her for the most part, just to be safe.

Chapter 12
"The Date"

Pacing outside the barn, Snow knew she was a few minutes early. Dressed in her favorite pink dress and wearing her honeysuckle perfume, she felt her butterfly friends flutter in her stomach. She even asked Stevie to 'bird-sit' Tweety for her, so nothing would disturb their date. Stevie promised Snow that he would not come to the barn for ANY reason. Mitch had told her to meet him in the barn at 6:00 that evening. OK, it's gotta be time, now. She felt like she'd waited forever.

She slowly opened the large creaky barn door, "Hello? Mitch?"

"Hello Snow, please come in." Mitch had prepared all day for the date that evening. He was determined that everything would be perfect. He had already warned the men that the barn was 'off-limits' for the night. Kristen graciously offered to take over dinner for the village so he could prepare the barn for he and Snow's date. Mitch had asked Bart to clean the barn especially well that day and promised to return the favor.

"Where are you?"

"I'm up here, sweet Princess."

She climbed the ladder to the hay loft to find there was no visible hay. Instead, on top of the hay there was a luscious layer of purple crushed velvet material that Mitch asked Jill if he could borrow for the evening. Sprinkled over the velvet were petals of wildflowers, Snow's favorite. Mitch was dressed handsomely in a dark colored sweater. Snow thought that these sweater garments looked especially nice worn by the men. Besides being warm and soft, they showed the broadness of their shoulders and thickness of their chests.

Laid out in front of Mitch were two covered dinner plates, and two empty wine glasses. Next to him, was a bottle of wine, a coffee pot and a basket with some other items. Encircling the entire loft were white candles. And in the air was a most pleasant scent ... it was vanilla. She would have expected the barn to smell like horses, but it didn't. It was overwhelming for Snow ... certainly the most romantic environment she had ever seen.

"Good evening. You look absolutely beautiful, Snow."

"Thank you, Mitch. You look quite handsome yourself." As they gazed into one another's eyes for a moment, she rubbed her hand through the velvet material, "This is so soft. And you added flower petals. You're so thoughtful."

"It's royal purple for royalty ... for you Princess. And here." In his hand was a wild daisy. He gently placed the stem through her hair under her pink ribbon next to her ear. Snow smiled, biting her lower lip as Mitch uncovered the dinner plates, "And ... we have steamed asparagus, baked eggplant, and fresh grilled trout. Plus, the finest wine in the village," as Mitch pulled out the wine bottle and began to open it. He poured them both a glass, "How about a toast." They both raised their glasses. "To your new life in the Willows ... may all your dreams come true."

Snow masked her surprise taking a sip of the wine. How did he know about her dreams? Did he hear it from one of the girls maybe? About the prince in her dreams?

Snow tasted the entrée, "This fish is delicious."

"Yes, Nicholas actually caught this trout since Edward is ... oh, I'm sorry. I didn't want to bring up anything upsetting."

"That's OK. I just hope he can participate in the bonfire tomorrow evening. I would hate for him to have to miss it. I feel so guilty about it all."

"Now stop that. You are not to blame at all. Besides, tonight we are to think of nothing negative, alright?"

"Alright, " Snow agreed with a smile. "It sure smells lovely in here ... surprisingly so."

"That's the vanilla scented candles. They are like regular candles but give off a scent of vanilla. They came in the last mysterious crate we received."

"It still puzzles me how you receive those mysterious crates, Mitch."

"Yes, it puzzles me too."

After feasting on the dinner, Mitch pulled out of the basket a special covered plate, "How about dessert?" He uncovered a luscious looking cheesecake covered in strawberries.

"Mitch that looks positively scrumptious!"

After dessert, Mitch put the dishes into the picnic basket. "Now, I have another surprise for you."

"Another one?"

"Yes. Follow me." Mitch made his way down the ladder, and Snow followed him. As she was about to reach the bottom, Mitch pulled her from the ladder by her waist spinning her around and around as she laughed and squealed.

"Sorry, I had to do that. I had such fun twirling you around the morning you came out of the woods, that I thought it would be twice as much fun under more relaxed circumstances. But, now for the surprise." Mitch walked over to a familiar black box and fidgeted with some buttons. Suddenly, music began to play from the box.

It was the same contraption that Rein had brought to the barn when she danced with him and he kissed her. She all but shuddered at the coincidence of Mitch doing the very same thing. But Mitch and Rein are nothing alike. Rein is haughty and demanding at times, where Mitch is loving and giving.

Mitch saw the distant look on Snow's face as she stared at the player, lost in thought. "Snow, are you alright?"

"What? Oh, yes. I'm sorry. I was just remembering, that's all."

"Remembering? I know you didn't have one of these back home."

"No, I was remembering when Rein brought me here to dance and he had borrowed that same music player. I'm sorry. I didn't mean to be so distant."

Mitch wore a somewhat shocked look. He definitely didn't want any aspect of their date to remind her of Rein ... that was for certain. He would rather turn the music off and 'hum' if he had to.

"Here, I'll just get rid of this, then. I don't want any haunting memories to ..."

Snow went to him and gently put her hand on his arm, "No, that's alright. Why don't we make a new memory, Mitch?"

He turned back to look at Snow. Her deep blue eyes along with her lovely smile spoke volumes. He couldn't help but to kiss her. He kept it short and tender then asked her to dance. The first few songs were cheerful waltzes that Mitch had to show her the steps to a few of them. The songs became much slower and he dared to pull her closer. Her eyes were at a level just under his chin. He lowered his head to kiss the side of her face, still holding one hand, and with the other on her waist.

Snow wanted to get lost in the music, the moment, but something kept invading her thoughts ... Kate. How did he feel about Kate? She couldn't shake it from her mind.

Mitch's thoughts were also racing. He wondered if he should mention it now? Was this a good time? Why not? It was as good a time as any. But he hadn't even thought about what he would say. Oh well, here goes.

"You know, I must tell you that although you said that you didn't want me to attend your wedding, I really did want to go. Although, the thing about it is, I wanted to ... be in it, you know? Um, I really don't know how to say this ..." Mitch swallowed hard.

Snow was still so lost in her own disturbing thoughts, she hadn't heard a word Mitch had just said, "Mitch, I must ask you something."

Mitch was somewhat relieved that his next statement had a reprieve, "Of course, Princess."

"I need to know about Kate."

Mitch pulled his head back to look at Snow, "Kate?"

"Yes. I know you have some sort of feelings for her. You had a date with her not too long ago, I know that. And I see you two quite often talking and laughing. I even noticed that it made Donnie uncomfortable ... and so that makes me feel a little strange as well, to see Donnie not his confident self."

She let go of Mitch and turned to walk toward 24-Carrots, "It's just difficult to follow your heart when your heart's desire is possibly following something else, or someone."

Mitch wanted to tell her the truth. He approached her and put his hand on her shoulder, "Snow, I do care for Kate, as a very good friend. And I won't lie to you. Before you came to the Willows, I did have a crush on her, a big one. I tried many times to get her to go on a date with me, mostly to no avail, except one time. I think my favorite excuse of hers was 'I have to wash my hair tonight.'"

"Snow giggled, "She actually said that?"

"Yeah. You'd think I'd get the hint, eh? I never asked again once you came. You shouldn't be jealous of Kate, Snow."

"Well, I didn't want to say I was jealous, but ..."

"Well don't be. You know I get pretty jealous, too sometimes ... of you and Stevie spending as much time as you do together."

Snow laughed out loud, "Me and Stevie? You're jealous of Stevie?"

"Well yes, because he gets to spend more time with you than I do. You're always up there alone with him in your treehouse. It drives me insane!"

"Stevie always wants to read me a book and I let him. It helps me sleep, anyway. That's all. There's nothing else."

"Well, then that's how you should look at Kate and I. She's like my Stevie in a way, I suppose."

Snow laughed again, "Kate is Stevie?"

Mitch raised his hands in surrender, "Please don't tell her I said that or she'll probably kill me! You know I just meant it as a comparison."

"Yes, I know," Snow eyed him teasingly.

Mitch took her hand, "Now, since we have that cleared up,

shall we dance some more?" The two resumed their position on the 'dance floor' as the song once again possessed a very slow pace.

Mitch remembered the statement he was about to make earlier and pondered whether or not he should try it again.

Suddenly, Snow's shoulders shook as she giggled, unable to hold it back any longer, "I'm sorry. I just still can't believe you're jealous of Stevie!"

Perhaps he should wait until next time to bring up the subject under the circumstances, Mitch thought.

After several more dances, both of them began to tire out. Mitch went back up to the loft to gather the dishes and blow out the candles. He would gather the velvet material and candles in the morning once they had cooled. He took the basket with one arm and Snow's arm with the other. As they walked back to her treehouse, they talked about the plans for the bonfire the next day. It should feel nice and warm with the chill in the air they felt now.

They reached the tree house and Mitch set down his basket. Snow turned into him, close. He put his arms around her waist and she wrapped hers around his neck. He looked into her eyes for a moment then kissed her gently. As he kissed her, he pulled her in closer for perhaps a more passionate kiss. At that moment, a cold breeze blew through the village and Snow shuddered.

Mitch slowly pulled out of the kiss and rubbed his arms up and down her back to warm her, "My, it's getting colder, isn't it? You should be inside where it's warm."

Snow sensed Mitch's disappointment, and in all trusting quietly offered, "Would you like to come up for a while?"

Although possibly the most tempting thought Mitch has had in a long time, he smiled, "No. I know it's late and you need your rest. But I had a lovely evening. I thank you for the wonderful privilege of your company, Princess." He took her hand and kissed it.

"Thank you ever so much Mitch. I had the most lovely evening ever!"

He made sure she was safely in her house before he left the foot of the tree and made his way home.

"Can I help you there?" came Snow's voice as Ivan was arranging the wood for the bonfire for that night.

"I don't know. Bart just went to take a break. I wouldn't want you to hurt yourself."

"Nah! And these are my work clothes, besides. How about I pass the wood to you from the wheel barrel?"

In a 'chain' type fashion, Snow passed Ivan log after log as he carefully put them in place for the fire.

"What do you miss most about back home, Ivanhoe?"

He thought for a moment, "Well, besides my family, I suppose I sort of miss walking through the town with all of the people selling their wares and such. Sometimes it's rather cheerful to be around a large crowd of people, although I wouldn't want that all the time, mind you. But that was the first thing that came to mind. How about yourself?"

"I miss the castle the most I think. I loved peering over all the balconies overlooking the countryside. My father has been gone over a year, so I found much comfort just roaming the large castle corridors and wondering what was around the next corner. When I was a child I would play that a dragon was around the corner and that a brave prince would be there to slay it and save me. Sounds silly, I know."

"No, it doesn't sound silly at all, Snow. It's actually very charming. And I would think that I would probably miss living in a castle myself. We had a very nice home. It wasn't a castle, but I do miss it sometimes, just the same."

"Did you fight in many battles?"

"Yes, actually. I reported directly to King Richard. We saw many battles, some faired victorious and others not so well."

Ivan shared some of his battles with Snow until Bart returned. In talking, the three soon discovered that they had quite a lot in common to talk about in customs and heritage. Bart mentioned finding the 'new world' with his brother, Christopher Columbus ... a concept almost unthinkable to Snow. She of course never imagined that there were any other lands out there so far away from her own ... that is until she woke up in Whispering Willows.

"You know, I've been thinking."

"'Bout what?" Jill replied, as Kate laid back on Jill's floor rug.

"About the woods. Ever since Snow came out of those woods alive after being out there all night. That crest of hers ... she said it protected her. She said it 'glowed'."

She sat up and looked at Jill, "I wonder if there would be any way to use it. You know, everyone's curious about that village on the other side of the mountain. I wonder if we could use it somehow. You think we could get out of the woods? Make it out alive at night?"

"That'd be somethin' you'd have to talk to Snow 'bout, Kate." Jill looked at Kate with much curiosity, "Why all the questions centerin' around leavin', Kate? You goin' somewhere?"

Kate laid back down, "No, just curious. That's all. Hey, has anything strange happened with Eddy, lately at all? He's been in that jail two days, now."

Jill sighed, "No, nothing has happened. He said he doesn't even get dizzy spells anymore."

Kate continued to stare at a spot on Jill's ceiling, "Maybe they can let him out. It's cruel to just leave him in there."

"Well, they're going to try one last test. They have to leave him alone with Snow."

Kate sat up again, "Alone with Snow? That's awfully dangerous. Isn't it?"

"Yes, but it's the only way to tell. Margurite always seemed to emerge when they were alone, mostly. Besides, Snow will stay on the other side of the bars and the men will be just outside the jail in case she yells. They're going to try it this afternoon so hopefully Eddy will be able to attend the bonfire tonight."

"Well, I sure want to be there for that, then."

Jill smiled, "Of course. Everyone does."

"Anything happen, Snow? Anything at all?" Duncan pressed.

"No. We were a little nervous about it at first ... not knowing if he would fly around the cell or what. But no, nothing. I never even saw him with green eyes, ever."

Kristen was concerned that Eddy wouldn't be able to make the bonfire that night, "Well, perhaps we could let him out and just keep a close watch on him, then ... at least for tonight."

Donnie shook his head, "I don't know."

Duncan offered to Donnie, "What if we assigned two men to be with him at all times. "

"Well, I guess that sounds OK. But at the first sign of trouble ... and I mean anything ... we gotta lock 'im up. Got it?"

The men let Eddy out and he and Snow smiled at each other. He walked on to his cabin with Thomas and Nicholas, the two men that agreed to stay with him. He wanted to get a good hot bath.

The sky was unusually clear that night. Snow swore she could see every star in the sky. How beautiful the fire looked in front of a black sky of stars. Mitch approached her with a tray of fresh rye bread. How does he do it? He can find time to cook just about anything! She took a piece of bread and held his gaze for a moment, flirtatiously. Maybe the 'flirting' tactic of Kate's is something she should try on Mitch more often. As Snow watched Mitch offering bread to the others, she noticed Jill snuggle up to Roger near the fire. There you go! Why couldn't that be she and Mitch? He is so giving, but at the same time, he is 'giving' to everyone else, leaving Snow sitting here all by herself.

She thought she might just go snatch that tray out of his hands and ... what's this? She noticed Mitch offering the bread to Kate and her all 'flirty-like'. There they go again! That 'flirt' thing! Golly! That's what I'm talking about, thought Snow. She glanced over and saw Stevie sitting, reading his book by the fire. OK, then. Fine. Two can play this game!

Snow quietly crept over to Stevie and snatched his book from his hands, "Whatcha readin', Stevie?" She danced around giggling and waving the book around out of his reach as he tried to get it. Seeing that this was a game, he played along, still trying to get the book back. Finally, as she turned to round the corner of the bonfire, he grabbed her around the waist, lifted her up, and twirled her around. Snow, still clinging to the book, was squealing and laughing.

Mitch caught the game out of the corner of his eye and set down his tray. Of course, it became an all too familiar scene when Stevie picked Snow up and twirled her around, as Mitch so loved to do.

Finally, Snow and Stevie both tumbled to the ground laughing. "I give! Here's your book, Stevie!" Snow stood up and made her way back to her seat still laughing and brushing the grass off of her dress.

She looked up to find Mitch eyeing her curiously, "What was that all about?"

Snow thought, hmm, looks like her plan worked like a charm. "Nothing. Just having a little fun with someone not so busy."

"'Not so busy', huh?" Just then Mitch dipped Snow as though he were about to kiss her. Snow, being embarrassed to kiss in public, playfully wriggled to get free. She succeeded, and as she landed a hard 'thud' on the ground, she began to laugh hysterically.

Mitch eyed her with raised eyebrows as he picked up his tray.

"Hey Mitch, you didn't slip her some of that homemade booze of yours, did ya?" laughed Nicholas.

Suddenly, there was a commotion on the other side of the bonfire with Kate and Donnie. Kate was shouting and hitting Donnie. As some of the others made their way over there to see what's up, Snow looked up into the smoke cloud above the bonfire. She screamed "It's her! It's her! She's there!"

Mitch was startled by her scream and dropped his tray of bread. He tried to help her up. She was crying and looked at Mitch. "NO! Green eyes! "Green!" she screamed. She shoved him away and fell back to the ground.

Mitch knelt down to try to comfort her. Ivan came over to assist him in helping her up. She was fighting the both of them.

"What is it? Is she OK?" Snow looked around to the voice. It was Edward. Snow gave a blood curdling scream and blacked out, falling to the ground.

Edward blinked his brown eyes from the bonfire's smoke. "She OK?"

Later, as Snow awoke and was moved off to the side of the commotion, she saw Kristen and Jill throwing bread into the fire. She saw many of the men fighting and was frightened. Mitch noticed she was awake and went over to meet her.

Some of the villagers had fallen victim to 'ergot poisoning', which is a parasitic fungus that thrives on rye under certain climate conditions. Symptoms can include hallucinations, among other things.

Kristen ran up to Mitch, "Is there any more bread in the kitchen? What about bread dough? We have to get rid of it!"

Snow coughed out, "Bread dough ... who 'kneads' it!" In catching her own pun, Snow laid back onto the grass laughing hysterically, kicking her feet into the air. Mitch peered down at her with a look of surrender.

"Why don't you let me take her home, Mitch?"

Mitch turned around, "Oh, Ivan, that would be so kind. I have so much to take care of to make sure no one else gets a hold of this 'stuff'."

"Sure. No problem. Donnie found Kate unconscious, and so he's taking care of her for now. I'll just make sure Snow gets home safely."

"I can't go up there! She's up there! She'll try and kill me!"

Snow trembled as she and Ivan stood at the foot of her tree house.

"Snow, you need to sleep this off. It's having a bad effect on many of us."

"But I can't go up there. I'm scared."

"Snow, there's no one up there."

"Can I stay with you?"

"I don't think Mitch would like that very much."

"Oh, Mitch-ShMitch. You can tell me about Robin Hood!"

"Oh, dear. It will take me a bit to explain this one, but ... I suppose."

As they began to make their way to Ivan's cabin, the tree-house door slowly opened. Peering down from the darkness were two small glowing lights ... green in color.

Ivan was supporting Snow's weight on his shoulder with her arm around his neck as they entered his cabin. "I guess it's the ol' chair for me tonight, eh." He chuckled as he gently set her down on the bed.

"Ivan, did you ever fight any dragons back home?" Her words were slurred as she rocked back and forth on the bed.

"Snow, there are no such things as dragons. Where did you hear that?" As he turned from adding wood to his fire, he found Snow slumped sideways on the bed, fast asleep. "There now. You just stay there and sleep this off. I hope there are no after effects for you in the morning."

It was difficult to fall asleep in his rather hard wooden chair, but as he watched the princess slumber, he smiled at her and soon found that slumber himself.

Chapter 13
"Powdered Kiss"

After thanking Ivan for his kindness in letting her stay in his cabin, Snow made her way home back to her treehouse. She didn't remember anything of the night before from the time after she returned Stevie's book to him in teasing him at the bonfire. Ivan had told her of the ergot poisoning in the bread that was served. Mitch must just feel terrible, Snow thought ... making bread that made people sick. She knew it wasn't his fault, but she knew Mitch pretty well nonetheless, and knew he must have felt badly about it. She made her way up the ladder and opened the door. She nearly stumbled over the obstacle in the kitchen area near the door. How sweet, Snow thought! Mitch must have left it for her last night. She would go right away and thank him in person for the lovely basket of fruit in her tree house. She grabbed the large red apple on the very top and headed down the ladder.

"No, sorry Mitch, " Thomas held his head to try and steady the dizziness he was still feeling, not to mention that his nose was still throbbing from the previous evening's fist fight. "With that ridiculous 'ergot' junk, I don't remember much about last night ... much less being able to keep an eye on Edward."

Mitch scowled and turned to Nicholas, "What about you? You two were supposed to keep an eye on Eddy last night. Now he's missing and has been all night, for all we know. Thank God Snow stayed with Ivan last night rather than alone in her tree house."

"She did?" Thomas said with the sound of a congested nasal

passage, "I thought you wouldn't be too happy about something like that."

"Well, Ivan said Snow had a bad feeling about going home from the beginning. Besides, Ivan is a gentleman. I trust him."

"What about the river?" Nicholas offered, "Maybe he's fishing this morning."

Mitch nodded, "Perhaps. Can you go and check? I'd like to go and see how Snow is. It's getting pretty late in the day."

Nicholas and Thomas both went to look for Eddy.

Mitch was taking off his apron when he heard a noise behind him. He turned to see Snow throwing an apple into the air and catching it.

"Good morning, you thoughtful sweetheart."

"Good morning, Snow. " She wore a huge smile that Mitch found exhilarating.

"You're such a dear. See, I even brought part of your gift with me."

"I'm not sure what you're talking about a 'gift', but I'm so glad to see you're looking well."

"Mitch, you can't fool me. I know you're just being humble. Would you like to share your gift with me?"

Mitch wore a baffled look, "Gift?"

"Now, are you going to just keep denying that you left me that beautiful basket of fruit in my treehouse last night, Mitch?" She started to take a bite out of the apple she had brought with her.

"Fruit? Snow, no!" He grabbed the apple out of her hand and threw it on the ground.

Snow stood confused.

"I didn't leave you a basket, and Edward is missing ... has been all night. I wouldn't want to take any chances on that fruit, Snow. OK?"

Snow looked down disappointed, "Alright. I understand."

Mitch realized and reached for her hand, "Snow, I'll give you a hundred baskets of fruit if you want me to, love."

Snow smiled and looked up, "Can I just have YOU in a basket?"

"You can have me anywhere, Snow."

Suddenly feeling a bit awkward, Snow inquired "Did you say that Edward was missing?"

"Yes, Nicholas and Thomas went to check on him."

"Ivan said this whole thing was caused by something wrong with the bread?"

Mitch rubbed her arm, "Ergot poisoning. Kristen told us about it."

"Do you know where she is? I'd like to ask her," Snow inquired.

"The girls are helping to tend to Kate. She didn't fair too well last night, either."

Nicholas gave a sigh of relief as he and Thomas came upon Edward at the river, "Here you are! We've been looking for you everywhere, Eddy!"

"Sorry, guys. I've been here."

"How long? We didn't see you all night."

"Don't know. I don't remember much about last night. Thomas, what happened to your face?"

"Long story. What do you mean you don't remember? Did the bread affect you too?"

"Bread?"

"Yeah, the rye bread that Mitch was passing around the bonfire. Kristen said it caused 'ergot poisoning'. They say it can give a person hallucinations and the like. A lot of people were really affected by it."

Edward shook his head, "I didn't eat any of the bread. I don't know what's going on. First thing I knew was that I woke up here. What if it's HER again? I decided to just stay here so I couldn't hurt anyone."

Nicholas and Thomas looked at each other. Nicholas gave Edward a quick stare to be sure his eyes were brown. "Let's go on back, Eddy. We need to tell the others."

"Well, at least let me catch something for dinner first. I can't hurt anyone out here."

"You sure Eddy?"

"Yeah, just give me a little while."

"Alright, we'll come back for you later, then."

Snow returned to her treehouse after getting the run down on ergot poisoning from Kristen. She sat on her couch pillows and admired the daisy she had put in a vase, the one that Mitch had put in her hair on their date the other night. She noticed one of the petals had fallen from it. She felt all 'grimy' from the bonfire last night, as she hadn't bathed yet. She knew Kate's cabin was out of the question and the others were probably already using their baths for the same purpose. Snow figured the best place to go would be the guest bath in the main hut. She grabbed a change of clothes and headed for the main hut.

When she arrived, it was all but deserted. The only one in the main cabin portion was Bart reading.

"Hello, Bart. Is that one of Stevie's books, there?" said Snow as she entered the hut with her clothes.

"Yes. I really didn't have anything better to do, believe it or not." He saw the clothes in her arms, and he winked at her playfully, "Mitch isn't here at the moment."

"That's alright. I'm just here to take a bath. I imagine all the others are occupied."

"Let me know if you need any help," he teased.

"Don't worry, I'll let you know." She giggled as she closed the door behind her and began to run the water in the tub. Good, it's warm, she thought. As she was about to undress, something caught her eye in the corner of the room. She approached the object on the floor next to the full-sized mirror. She gasped, then calmed herself. I'm sure that's just a similar looking jar. That can't be the same one. Donnie buried it in the woods. As she picked up the empty jar, it felt dusty in her hands. She quickly set it down and brushed off her hands. The dust that was on her hands was brown. It was not dust at all, it was dirt. It was as if the jar had been ... dug up?

As she stood up, she was facing the mirror. The reflection she saw took her breath away. She was frozen in terror. She couldn't speak, she couldn't scream. It was her! She was there in the mirror! But it can't be! Maybe it's the ergot. Snow turned around. She gasped. There was Edward with those haunting green eyes. She hadn't heard anyone come in. The door was still closed. She shut her eyes and turned back to the mirror. She was still there! Edward's reflection in the mirror was not Edward ... it was the queen, Margurite!

"What do you mean he's gone?"

Duncan raised his hands, "Wait, let me get this straight. You found Eddy at the river. He didn't remember anything before waking up in the woods ... anything about last night, and he admitted to not eating any of the bread. And you left him there? Then you came back for him later and he was gone ... IS gone!"

"We looked everywhere," as Thomas sat down on a large chair in the main hut.

Mitch quickly asked, "Where is Snow?"

Bart glanced up from his book, "She just went in to take a bath a minute ago, just before you lads came in."

A terrified scream came from the direction of the guest bath. All of the men went running toward it. Mitch threw open the door to see Snow in Edward's grasp. He had her arms in his grip and was pushing her toward the mirror. As he looked in their direction, they saw those dreaded green eyes. Edward went to shove Snow into the mirror. Mitch lunged to try to stop him from crashing her head into the glass. To his surprise and everyone else's, Snow and Mitch went right through the mirror as if it were an open window, disappearing. Edward fell to the ground, coughing. He hadn't gone into the mirror. Duncan ran to the mirror, but saw nothing but his own reflection.

He called out, "Mitch! Snow!" Nothing ... no reply. Duncan and Nicholas picked Eddy up as he held his head, staggering.

He looked at Duncan with his brown eyes, "What happened?"

"The queen! That's what happened. She was here again."

"Wait a minute!" Shouted Nicholas, "What the devil happened to Mitch and Snow? They just disappeared."

"I don't know."

Nicholas went running out of the hut to check the side of the building to see if they had come out the other side. "Are they gone forever?"

Duncan shook his head, "I'm not sure, Thomas. I wish I knew what was going on myself."

"Look at this." Thomas picked up the jar sitting next to the mirror. "Isn't this the same jar that Donnie buried in the woods that had the broken mirror shard in it? It's empty."

Duncan ran his hand over the surface of the mirror for any sign of them. There was nothing. Just a cold piece of glass.

Kristen's, Yolanda's and Jill's jaws dropped as Duncan told them what happened in the guest bath.

"We're getting a team together and are going to begin searching everywhere. I've not told Donnie. I'd rather wait until Kate wakes up at least. He has a lot to worry about right now. I'd appreciate it if the rest of you would not tell him just yet."

The others nodded. The team was made up of Duncan, Nicholas, Thomas, Bart and Stevie. Mainly, because they saw what happened, and Stevie because he may have a lot of insight to where Snow could be. Their first stop would be the place in the woods where Stevie found Snow. There were a lot of mysterious occurrences around that area, such as Snow seeing the strange mist. Besides, since they found the jar in the bath that was supposed to have been buried in that spot in the woods, they figured that it was the best place to start. They had to hurry, as it would get dark fairly soon. They took two horses and the remaining three went on foot.

"'ere ... this is it, guys!" Stevie called to the others when he reached the clearing where he had found Snow.

"Mitch! Snow!" The men started calling out as they looked

around.

"Over here, guys! We need help! We're over here!" The men followed the voice in the woods to where Mitch was sitting ... his head bleeding and an unconscious Snow lying in his arms.

"Mitch, thank God!" Duncan kneeled down to him, "What happened, man?"

It was apparent that Mitch had been crying, "I pulled her away, and we landed over there in those leaves." He pointed to a spot just meters away ... the very spot Stevie found the original mirror shard.

"It was like nothing I'd ever seen. One second, I'd lunged for Snow and Eddy, and the next second we were in this strange room, like a basement. And there were all these bottles on tables with colored liquids and smoke coming out of them. And then I looked and saw that Margurite had Snow clenched in her hands instead of Eddy's. She had these long hideous fingernails. She dug them into Snow's arms making her cry, begging her to stop."

Mitch rubbed her arms where there were multiple red cuts on both of them, then he wiped a tear with the back of his hand, "I looked back and saw the place where we had come. It was a mirror. I could see all of you in the guest bath, even Eddy. I could hear you calling me. Next to that mirror was another mirror where I could see the woods. The lunge from the mirror had knocked me off my feet. When I got up, this huge black crow attacked me." He reached up to his forehead and touched his head where it was bleeding.

"I knocked the crow across one of the tables and got up. When I did, I saw Margurite blowing some sort of powder into Snow's face. She started coughing and wheezing and then she fell to the floor, grabbing the queen's dress for support. The queen shoved her away laughing. Snow fell towards me. The first thing I could think of was to grab her and jump through that mirror where I could see the woods. That's what I did."

Mitch began crying, "But I can't wake her up. She must have put some kind of spell on her with whatever that powder was.

She won't wake up." He lifted her head and gently patted her face and hands, "Snow? Princess?" He pulled her into him and gently stroked her hair, "We have to do something, we have to get her to the village and break this spell."

Duncan turned to Bart, "Untie the horses and bring them over here." Bart brought the horses. They put Mitch holding Snow on one of them and headed back to the village.

"No, not with the women. I want her with me." Mitch instructed as they reached the village.

"Look, it's Mitch! An' he's got Snow!" pointed Jill as the men came into view of the Willows.

They helped Mitch get Snow into bed. "I don't care if I have to sleep in a chair for a week, she's staying here," Mitch protested to Kristen and Yolanda's urgings that she stay with one of them.

"Let's try some water. Anyone gots any smellin' salts?" inquired Jill as Yolanda went to get some water.

"I think Kate might have some in her cabin."

"No Mitch. We just went through her cabin and there was nothing like that in there. What about something from the kitchen? Any ammonia?"

Mitch draped an extra blanket over Snow, "There's some with the cleaning supplies in the storeroom."
Bart came back with the ammonia. They tried it, but to no avail.

Mitch was raving, "That witch! That's it! I'm going back to the main hut. If I can get back through that mirror, I'm gonna kill her!"

Jill gently squeezed his arm, "Mitch, calm down..."

"Wait, where's Eddy? This is his fault anyway! He should be..."

Jill grabbed his arm harder this time, "Mitch!! Calm down! This isn't helpin'! Mitch, ya wanna be strong for Snow. She needs ya right now, dear. She might be able ta hear ya, ya know. That kind of stuff happens all th' time. People in comas an' stuff can hear their loved ones talkin' to 'em."

Kristen put her hand on Mitch's shoulder, "Perhaps she just needs to sleep it off. I'm sure in the morning she'll be bright-eyed as usual."

Mitch wanted Kristen's words to be true so badly he could taste it.

That evening, the others left Mitch to care for Snow. Mitch brushed her cheek with his hand. He touched her soft rosy lips. He constantly checked to make sure she was still breathing.

He whispered, "Snow, I can't lose you. Please come back to me." He could feel himself begin to cry, but he didn't want to do that. In the small possibility that she could hear him, he didn't want anything to dash her hopes, "Can you hear me, Princess? I don't know if you can, but there's something I want to tell you. I wanted to tell you the other night on our date, but it just didn't seem to be the right time. We were talking about Kate and Stevie and ... Snow, I wanted to tell you that I love you. Well, not just that, but ... your wedding. What I was trying to say was ... I wanted to be there ... but be in it, be part of it." He paused and took her hand, "I wanted to be the one marrying you, Snow. It should have been me, not Edward. I'm not sure how, but it should have been. I wanted to tell you all of this so badly. I know I should have told you the other night in the barn but ... well I just should have, that's all there is to it. I wish I would have, Snow. So, you see Princess, you have to wake up so I can tell you in person ... well, when you're awake. Fairy Princess, I AM your prince after all. Well, I really want to be ... not for just a costume, but in real life, Princess." Again, he fought back the urge to cry, "Sweet Princess, come back to me." Sitting next to her, he laid his head next to her hand. And as he breathed her in, he fell asleep.

The next morning, Mitch was awakened by a knock at his door.

Stevie came bounding into Mitch's cabin, "Any news?" He was followed by Jill and Kristen.

"She's still out. She didn't move a muscle all night long. I'm so worried about her." He realized, "You know, in all of this insanity, I totally forgot about supper last night."

"It was taken care of ... don't ya worry. Kristen here just baked some potatoes and served the fixin's 'buffet style', " smiled Jill. "But ya must be starved yourself. Why doncha let us go get ya somethin' ta eat, Mitch?"

"No, but thanks. I can't eat. Not with her like ... this."

"Mitch, ya know I just remembered something last that I wanted to tell ya," chirped Stevie excitedly. "In the story 'Snow White' when the queen put a spell on her, you know it was the prince who kissed her an' woke her up! Maybe Eddy could ..."

Mitch interrupted, "No way! That's ridiculous! I'm not letting that monster anywhere NEAR Snow!"

"Wait," thought Kristen. "Stevie has a point. Maybe we SHOULD go and get Eddy? It couldn't hurt to try. We'll all be here to make sure nothing bad happens."

"No. Something bad could still happen ... DID happen! You don't know what she's capable of!"

"Wait a minute." Jill stopped them. "Didn't ya say that ya fought the queen in the mirror? She was with you an' Snow, an' yet ya saw Eddy still back in th' bath with Duncan and th' others, right?"

"Well, yes."

"Well then I think maybe Eddy's not taken over by th' queen no more then."

"But Jill, I'm not willing to take that chance."

Kristen folded her arms, "Then perhaps you'd rather take the chance that Snow will sleep forever and ever. Is that what you want?"

Mitch sighed and looked at Snow, "Where is he, anyway?"

"They locked him back up after what happened. He's in the jail."

Without turning his eyes away from the Princess, "Alright. But I'm not leaving."

Edward entered the cabin cautiously. He saw Mitch standing

by Snow. When he turned and saw Eddy, he had to turn and walk away to try and hide his anger.

"Mitch, I'm so sorry. I didn't mean to hurt anyone. It was her. You know I would never do anything to hurt Snow."

Mitch kept his eyes away, "Yes, Edward, I know. I'm just upset about this whole thing is all. And the idea of you kissing Snow isn't helping matters."

Eddy looked at Kristen. She nodded. Edward approached Mitch's bed where Snow lay motionless. Mitch couldn't help but to turn and watch over this particular event. Edward leaned down to kiss Snow. He gently kissed her. Nothing happened.

Edward looked at Kristen. She shrugged, "I don't know. Maybe it takes a minute."

"No, no. I know wha' it is!" Stevie strided over to their side of the room. "In th' story, she was awakened by th' kiss of 'true love'. The prince was her true love in the story, but it doesn't necessarily have to be a 'prince' to wake up our Snow, right? It just needs to be her 'true love'."

Edward turned and looked at Mitch, "I agree. This is your job, mate!"

Mitch looked around at the others who were smiling and nodding. He slowly approached where the sleeping princess lay, as Edward crossed back to the door. Mitch swallowed ... not that he had any saliva left at that point. He looked at her face, that angelic face. Her eyes ... he so wanted to see her beautiful blue eyes again. Mitch leaned down to her face, slowly. He hesitated, then gently kissed her.

Chapter 14
"The Portal"

Although it was always a sweet experience to kiss Snow, this particular kiss was not one of the most enjoyable ones. Mitch was too scared ... scared that she wouldn't wake. And then what? What would wake her? He lifted his head from her lips and watched her. Nothing ... no movement.

Mitch touched her cheek, "Snow?"

Kristen touched Mitch's shoulder, "Maybe it takes a minute."

"No," he turned to Kristen, "I knew it was too good to be true. Her life may have been based on a fairy tale, but obviously it's not one anymore. What if I've lost her ... forever?"

"Mitch, nonsense. I'm sure that we can find the answer."

"Where? What else can we possibly do?"

"Well, pancakes sound good. I'm really quite hungry."

Mitch whirled around on one foot at the sound of her voice. At that moment he saw the two most beautiful blue eyes he's ever seen looking back at him ... and that warm, friendly smile of Snow's directed solely at him.

"Snow!" He choked, then dropped onto the bedside and took Snow into his arms and held her tightly. He held her so tightly, Snow had to make an extra effort to breathe. But she would never complain ... she simply laughed.

The room cheered. "OK, let's go get those pancakes for Snow." Kristen announced as she began shooing everyone out of the cabin to leave Mitch and Snow alone.

"That means you too, Stevie," as he stood smiling at the two ... happy to see that his friend was alright.

As the last guest left the cabin, Mitch took Snow's face in his hands and looked into her eyes, "Snow, I cannot tell you how scared I was. I was afraid you wouldn't wake up. I was afraid I'd lost you forever. I don't know what I'd do, Snow. I don't. What would I do if I couldn't see your smiling beautiful face every day? Hear your singing, look into your eyes, touch your skin?"

He took her hands in his. They both had tears in their eyes, "Snow, do you remember what happened in the guest bath and then in the mirror?"

She nodded, "I was so frightened. Then I dreamed she was coming after me the whole time, that is, except when I heard your voice, Mitch ... only I'm not sure if I wasn't dreaming that too."

"I did talk to you Snow. I'm sure you weren't dreaming. What did I say in your dream?"

Snow lowered her eyes, "Um, well, lots of things, really."

Mitch raised her head with his hand, "Like?"

She stuttered, "Like ... that you wanted me to come back. And ... you mentioned our date in the barn, I think."

"Is that all?"

"Well ..." Snow felt a shudder of fear in remembering Margurite. She grabbed Mitch and hugged him, "Please hold me for a while, my love. I'm frightened. I can still see her in my head. She'll be back for me, Mitch. I know she will. I can feel it."

"I'm not letting go of you, Snow. And I'm not letting you stay alone. You'll stay here with me until we know she's gone forever, alright Snow? I can't stand to see you afraid, my Princess." He held her for a while and rocked her back and forth. He had to find a way to destroy the queen. He and Snow would never have peace, never have happiness until Margurite was gone. He pulled back to look at her. He wanted to comfort her, to make her feel safe and not frightened. He smiled and rubbed his nose on hers, then rested his cheek against hers.

Snow felt like warm honey was running all through her as she closed her eyes to savor the moment with her 'true love'. But she had to know if her dreams had been true. Had those things she heard really happened or were they all in her head?

She dared to break the moment to ask, "How did you wake me from Margurite's spell?"

Mitch pulled back and looked at her, "It was Stevie who reminded us that the kiss from Snow White's 'true love' awakened her in the fairy tale ... the tale we are all so fascinated with because it is your life's story," he chuckled.

Then it really happened, Snow thought. She had heard every word in her slumber ... every word as it had been spoken in true life. She heard Stevie, Kristen, Jill ... and Mitch. She had heard all that he said about her, about Edward, about the barn, about the wedding ... their wedding. He wants to marry her! She desperately wanted to tell him. She remembered his regret that he hadn't told her his feelings in the barn.

She didn't want to regret not telling him as well. "Mitch, I-"

"Here we go! Pancakes per your request!" Stevie cheerfully burst in holding a tray with two breakfast plates of pancakes and syrup.

"Knock, Stevie. You're supposed to knock! Sorry about that." Kristen said apologetically as she followed him into the cabin.

"Aye, sorry. But I know ya said ya were hungry." He set the tray on the bed.

"Yes, Stevie. Thank you, I am." Snow smiled as she pulled the tray up closer.

"OK, Stevie. Let's go have breakfast ourselves. See you two later."

Mitch added as they were leaving, "Thanks for everything, Kristen."

She smiled as she closed the door behind her. Snow tried her best to eat slowly so as not to look like a pig in front of Mitch. She was just so famished. At one point Mitch noticed a bit of syrup on her lip. Too enticing to resist her already sweet lips now covered with maple syrup, he boldly reached up, put his hand behind her neck and pulled her in to kiss her. He surrounded her lips with his, gently licking the syrup from them. Taken by surprise, Snow halfway wanted to respond to such a passionate kiss from Mitch, but was too preoccupied with wanting to get rid of her mouthful of pancakes ... not too appealing she would imagine, for a kiss of passion. She giggled and pulled back, covering her mouth as she chewed and swallowed the pancakes. Gosh, she wished she weren't so darn hungry! Is this what Jill meant by men being in the 'mood' in the mornings?

"Sorry, Princess. You're just too sweet to resist." Mitch let her finish the rest of her breakfast in peace.

Finally, she had gotten her bath, Snow thought as she entered her treehouse after having bathed at Jill's after breakfast. She giggled as she remembered Mitch arguing with Jill about not leaving her side, even for her bath! Gee, I wonder if there was an ulterior motive there, she thought. "Nah!" She said to herself sarcastically. She noticed that the fruit basket had been removed from her house, and in its place was a bag of homemade cookies from 'you know who'.

"Goodness, I guess he's trying to get me fat, replacing fruit with cookies!" she laughed. "Oh, poor daisy." She then sadly noticed the flower Mitch had given to her on their date had lost three more petals. "I wish you could live forever." She dug into the bag of cookies. She simply couldn't resist sweets, especially Mitch's. Along with the cookies she found a rolled piece of paper. She unrolled the note and something fell to the ground. It was a bracelet. She picked it up. It was handmade of coffee beans ... each one hand painted a different color. It smelled wonderful, like Mitch's coffee. The note read: 'To my true love. You will forever be in my heart. Love, Mitch' She slipped it on immediately and then dashed off to find him in order to thank him 'properly'.

Mitch was just finishing the dishes. It was the least he could do after the ladies made the breakfast for everyone so he could spend that time with Snow. Suddenly, an arm was wrapped around his neck from behind him. The arm wore the bracelet of coffee beans and he rubbed it.

He turned around to face her and she lifted the bracelet to her lips and kissed it, "Thank you for such a beautiful gift, much better than a basket of fruit."

He in turn took her hand and also kissed it.

"Do you know why I shall cherish my new bracelet?"

"Why?" he smiled.

"Because it was handmade by my true love."

She put her arms around his neck and moved in closer to him, her face only centimeters from his, "Do you know what else?"

Mitch shook his head.

"No pancakes this time." She smiled and leaned in to kiss him. With his arms around her waist, he pulled her closer into the kiss.

"Oi, Mitch I found some more dishes in the cabin. Sorry, I guess I just missed them."

Snow pulled back, giggling. Well, she thought. It was bound to happen, always does. Mitch didn't look so amused as he took the dishes from Stevie with a muffled 'thanks' through clenched teeth. Stevie bounced back out the door and into the dining hall. OK, so the kitchen was obviously not the place for ... well anything really, thought Mitch. Perhaps it's time for another date. That evening he had already made plans for the dinner for everyone, but tomorrow night? Yes, perfect. That was the night.

He would tell her everything. "Snow, do you have any plans tomorrow night?"

Snow side-glanced him flirtatiously, "No."

"Well, how about dinner at my cabin, then? There is much we need to talk about."

"There is, huh?" she asked, knowingly.

"Yes, Princess. There is." He took her hand with her bracelet and kissed it.

There was a soft knock at the door. Eddy peeked his head in cautiously, "Hello, just wanted to get a coffee refill."

"It's alright Eddy, you can come on in." Mitch poured him a refill. Edward gave them both a friendly smile and promptly left.

Snow turned back to him, "I'm glad they let him out of the jail."

Mitch sighed, "Yes. It wasn't fair to leave him in there. Besides, I think there is truth to what Jill said to me. Since we had Margurite with us in the mirror, and Eddy was left behind in the bath, I really do think he is free of her."

"So where do you think she is now?"

"Well, I'm hoping she is still in the portal, because that's how I'm going to get rid of her."

Snow gasped with concerned surprise, "You are? How?"

"Don't worry about it, Princess. I don't want you to be afraid, alright?"

"But I am worried, Mitch. Whatever you're thinking, I'm sure it's dangerous. You have to tell me or I'll just be sick with worry."

He kissed her forehead, "Alright."

Mitch went over and pulled a small canvas bag out of the back of one of the drawers. Out of the bag he pulled out a bundle wrapped in a large dishrag. He unwrapped the dishrag to display an oblong-like shaped object. It was an avocado green and was very bumpy. Snow reached out to touch it. It was cold and hard, like metal.

"Careful, this is a dangerous object."

"It looks almost like a vegetable."

"Yes, I know. But believe me, it isn't. It's called a 'grenade'. You mustn't say anything. If Donnie knew I had it, he'd kill me."

"How'd you get it?"

"There were a bunch of them in one of the 'mysterious' crates. Donnie usually gets them all, but he missed this one. I thought we should have one that wasn't in his possession, just in case of an emergency. Well, to me this seems like an emergency."

"How does it work? How can you use it to get rid of Margurite?"

Mitch demonstrated, "You pull this pin out, throw it as far as you can toward your target, then run and duck for cover, because after a few seconds it will explode."

"Explode?!"

"Yes, therefore blowing up the portal itself. She can't come back if her doorway is gone. There has been plenty of rain, so there shouldn't be any fear of fire."

Snow stood wide-eyed at the thought of 'blowing-up' any part of the woods.

Mitch took her face in his hands, "I know it's a bit extreme, Snow. But I don't want this woman coming between us anymore. You mustn't say anything to anyone. You know this is something they wouldn't allow."

"But this could get you into terrible trouble with Donnie and Duncan and everyone."

"I know. That's alright. Besides, it's always better to ask forgiveness than permission, you know." He laughed.

"When will you go?"

"Tomorrow after breakfast. Then nothing will spoil our date. By then, I'll have things all settled with Donnie and the others."

"Optimistic, aren't you? I'm going with you. Then they can blame us both."

"No, absolutely not. It's too dangerous, Snow. You're not coming with me."

"But Mitch, it's dangerous for you too."

"I know. But you've never handled one of these before."

"Have you?"

"No."

"Well, then?"

"Snow..."

"How do you know she's still in the portal?"

"Well, I don't. I just hope she is. I'm pretty sure that she has to have a medium to travel through, like the mist you saw, or the mirror shard that Stevie found. That's how she got into the village, and proceeded to take over Eddy. Donnie already shattered and disposed of the large mirror in the guest bath, so I don't think she'll be coming back through there. She's there waiting for us in the portal, waiting for you. That's why I can't let you go with me. You're staying here where it's safe. I love you. I have to make sure you're safe."

He kissed her forehead again and wrapped up the grenade, "Well, I guess I'll finish up these last minute dishes that Stevie brought."

"Snow?" Stevie returned to the kitchen. Speaking of Stevie, Snow thought.

"I've got Tweety, 'ere. I forgot all about 'im. I was goin' ta give him to ya earlier. I took really good care of 'im."

"Tweety! Thank you Stevie." She lovingly cradled the bird and kissed its head. "Are you ready to go home, Tweety? Let's go." As she carried her pet out of the kitchen, Mitch looked on with just a hint of envy that Tweety was going home with Snow, and he was not.

Even though Mitch wanted her to stay with him until the issues with Margurite could be resolved, Snow insisted that she stay in her treehouse. She'd keep the whistle nearby, but she didn't feel right about staying alone with him. Although, she wanted to very much, she was afraid of what the others might think about it. That evening, as she watched her little bird flutter about in her couch pillows, it reminded Snow how the butterflies would flutter in her stomach so very often, especially when she was with Mitch. But they weren't there now. She was nervous, worried.

"Tweety, I'm so worried about Mitch. I don't want him going out there in those woods without me ... with HER out there, ready to pounce. I got everyone into this mess in the first place. I need to get them out." She plopped back onto the pillows. "I'm the one she followed here. I should be the one to get rid of her." She thought for a moment as she turned her beloved bracelet around and around on her wrist, smelling its rich fragrance. "That's it then. I shall take care of this myself. I'm not afraid of her, anymore. I'm too angry, now." She sat up to see her daisy had lost two more petals, and it irritated her all the more. She stomped up to her bed loft and turned in early. She had a big day the next day.

Snow awoke early, before dawn, and got dressed. "You stay here. This is a dangerous mission, Tweety." She crept down her ladder and made her way to the main hut, careful that no one saw her. Just as she suspected, there was no one there. She quickly went into the kitchen and pulled out the drawer. Good, it was there! She grabbed the bag and carefully put it into her knapsack for her journey.

She took her time slowly as she made her way to the portal in the woods. She wasn't quite sure if it were due to her uneasiness to return to that spot or because she wanted to scope the woods for the queen's presence anywhere. There it was ... the clearing! She stopped just short of it when she saw it ... the mist. Margurite was still there. She didn't dare enter the clearing. She quickly fumbled through her bag for the grenade. She carefully held it in her hand wondering how large of a 'blow' would it cause? How much time would she have to run for cover? It didn't matter. The portal would be gone ... the queen would be gone. She put her finger through the pin and pulled.

"I knew I should have locked the thing up, " thought Mitch as he ran to the spot in the woods where he knew Snow had gone. When he found the grenade missing that morning, he knew what had happened. It was his own fault, he should never have shown it to her. He should have known she would try and remedy the situation herself. He knew how guilty she felt about bringing Margurite to the Willows. He just hoped he could get to her in time ... get to her before she used it. He hoped he could get to her alive.

Afterword

Finally, I want to thank you the reader, for coming along on this ride. I hope you had as much fun as I did, and enjoyed getting to know the heroes and heroines of Whispering Willows. If so, please take a moment to post a review and tell a friend. I would love to read your review!

The adventures are just beginning, so if you'd like to follow along, and get notifications of new releases and special offers on my books, please join my email list by going to www.DianaDawnBooks.com or drop me a line at Diana@DianaDawnBooks.com. I'd love to hear your thoughts. Thank you and happy reading!

Books In This Series

Whispering Willows

Check out the next book in the series!

Forget Me Not

For a FREE copy, visit
http://dianadawnbooks.com/free/

After falling into a magical world called the Whispering Willows, Snow has found new friends and her "Prince Charming". But her wicked stepmother is still after her. If she is to find any peace in her new life, she must find a way to destroy the evil witch...a way that will not endanger her new friends or herself in the process. 'Forget Me Not' is the second book in the Whispering Willows series.

CPSIA information can be obtained
at www.ICGtesting.com
Printed in the USA
LVHW041913081220
673650LV00003B/443